FALLS
LIKE
LIGHTNING

Books by
Shawn Grady

Through the Fire

Tomorrow We Die

Falls Like Lightning

SHAWN GRADY

FALLS LIKE LIGHTNING

BETHANYHOUSE
Minneapolis, Minnesota

Published by Bethany House Publishers
11400 Hampshire Avenue South
Bloomington, Minnesota 55438

Bethany House Publishers is a division of
Baker Publishing Group, Grand Rapids, Michigan.

Printed in the United States of America

ISBN 978-1-61129-953-3

For my wife

For where your treasure is, there will your heart be also.
Luke 12:34 KJV

CHAPTER 01

Heaven banished Lucifer in one air-rending fissure.

Silas Kent drew little difference—again at the doorway, one foot from the slipstream, four thousand over a crowning inferno. He closed his eyes and inhaled the oily scents of burnt pine and juniper whipping through the crew compartment. The engine roar blended into background. Convective heat buzzed at his cheeks, waving off the firestorm below. The mountain plateau lay like an altar, burnt offerings shadowed beneath its smoky pall.

The pilot tapped a dash gauge in the cockpit. The yoke vibrated and he returned his hand to it. Warren emerged from the fore bulkhead and rubbed the gray stubble at his jawline. His eyes found Silas and he gave the nod.

Once more unto the breach. Cast toward the earth and the blackened soil.

Warren slid on his sunglasses and took a knee by the jump door. He pointed to a clearing. Silas noted the spot, flipped down the caged face mask on his helmet, and gave the thumbs-up. No words needed save for the count-off that followed.

Three.

Hands on the doorframe.

Two.

Foot on the threshold.

One.

Silas barreled through the open air.

His chute deployed with a fabric slide and billowed jerk. Breath escaped his chest. He adjusted his joints and settled in the harness.

Alone with the wind. The great expansive ecstasy.

He angled toward the drop zone, the only suitable spot within hiking distance of the radio tower where an injured technician lay. A billowing column grew from the forest nearby. He mapped the fire in his mind, taking mental pictures of its size and perimeter, making out the shape of the radio repeater perched atop a wooded knoll. The closest rescue-equipped helicopter faced an hour and a half response time. Chances were that by the time it arrived the lack of visibility from the smoke would hamper efforts.

At its current rate of spread, the fire threatened to crest the ridge before Silas's team could get there.

Silas sighted the meadow clearing Warren had aimed him toward. Earth approached fast. He brought his boots together, hit the ground, and rolled. In one motion he made his knees and gathered in his chute arm over arm.

He breathed in the smell of earth and evergreen and burning sage.

Fifty feet from him, chute flapping, Peña landed and rolled. Silas shook down his jumpsuit, shouldered his fireline pack, and strode to the clearing edge.

Their window was slim. If winds picked up late that afternoon, and they always did, the opportunity for rescue would narrow even further.

"Rock."

A soccer-ball-sized stone tumbled down the hillside. Silas tucked his helmet and watched it bounce past him. Warren led the way, having made the jump with them this time instead of remaining with the plane as the team's spotter usually did. The spotter generally coordinated logistics and made sure the jumpers and their tools and supplies all got to where they needed to be, at the right time. Once he tapped their legs and sent them out the door, he kept in constant communication and coordinated their pickup. A spotter wasn't like a foreman on a hotshot crew. He didn't play the role of drill sergeant or lieutenant. He was a jumper, like them, and held the respect that years and experience provided.

Smoke swept up the hill around them, weaving between bushes and trees, funneling from the draw below. Their crew had been hoofing it since they hit the ground, racing the head of the fire toward the repeater and the downed technician. Victim rescue was a bit outside their normal job description. But if not them, then who? Silas drove the handle of his Pulaski axe into the dirt and continued the steep trek. Shaped similarly to a pick-head axe, the Pulaski sported a flat grubbing end opposite the axe blade to use as a hoe.

The eighteen Watch Out Situations drilled into him by the U.S. Forest Service echoed in his head.

Cannot see main fire, not in contact with anyone who can.

His eyes stung and watered from the smoke.

Terrain and fuels make escape to safety zones difficult.

He thought of the lectures he'd sat through about Storm King Mountain and the fourteen firefighters who lost their lives and how the instructor listed off the Watch Outs that were in violation leading up to the tragedy. Silas was in no mood to become a statistic. He pushed his quadriceps harder, digging his boots into the hillside to make a staircase for the guys behind him.

Static chirped from the King radio brick strapped to the pouch across his chest. Warren's voice carried. "Radio Tech Three, this is Redding Jumper Crew, how do you copy?"

Still no reply.

Per the last report before the crew had gone airborne, the radio tech had broken his leg in several places after a fall and possibly struck his head in the process. His last radio transmissions came across broken and confused. He was outside of cell service, didn't have a satellite phone, and without further radio communication there was no way to know if he was still conscious.

Silas gripped the trunk of a young pine. Shale slid under his boots.

"Chocolate pudding."

The phrase bumped its way down the line. In summers past, after long dry-throated hours working in the heat and dirt, the phrase *Watch your footing* had made the easy audible jump. Out of the eight men on their northern California–based smokejumper crew, Silas hiked second from the front—behind Spotter Warren Adams. Shouldering a chainsaw in the back, JD bore the brunt of the tumbling objects.

Warren secured a grip on the edge of a granite outcropping and pulled himself up. Silas scaled the same ledge. Along the mountainside the stone jutted straight up, stretching out in a broad bulwark. Their safest route would be to hike along the side slope, winding up the mountain until they could round above the granite cliff. Slow going at best.

Warren cocked his head, listening.

Silas peered into the smoky draw below. "What is it?"

He put a hand up. "Something's . . . This isn't . . ."

The smoke swirled. A strong wind rushed up the canyon. Silas braced his footing.

Warren gripped the rock face. "Fire's making a run."

"It'll bump that tower before we can get there."

Warren glanced from the gully to Silas, lips pressed tight. "All right. What's our LCES?"

Silas tied a bandana around his neck. "Lookouts—you're the eyes. Communications—line-of-sight radio com with HTs."

Warren set his goggles in place. "Good. Escape routes and Safety zones?"

"Down the opposite side of the hill, away from the fire."

"Won't help if we can't reach the top before it."

"Sidestepping along this hill isn't going to be fast enough."

Twisting clouds of smoke and dust veiled the rest of the crew below.

"No other way."

"We won't make it."

Silas turned to the sheer rock face. He ran his gloves over the granite and swallowed. This wasn't springtime top-roping with buddies. There was a definite difference between recreational rock climbing and stupid defiance of the forces of physics.

But that tech lay in the fire's path and time was running short.

His fingers found a hold. Two more broad crevices emerged overhead.

He could do it.

He unlaced his boots.

Warren knelt at the rock edge, cupping his hands to converse with Peña and Tran standing in the smoke below. "All right." He stood. "Here's what we're—What're you doing?"

Silas tied bootlaces around a shoulder strap of his fireline pack. "I think I can make it up."

Warren slashed his hand through the air. "Absolutely not. Put your White's back on."

"It'll take a fraction of the time." He shook off his pack and strapped his Pulaski to it. "I was first out of the plane, right? That makes me jumper in charge."

"And I'm your spotter. Leave it."

"Warren, you know we should already be there. Come on, I've free climbed walls much worse than this."

Yeah, right. Silas watched to see if he'd buy it.

Warren gazed at the rock wall and made a face like he'd stubbed his toe. He exhaled. "All right. But if you get in a tight spot, don't push it. Just climb back down. I'll leave Tran and Peña here to make sure you get to the top. Once you're up, they'll hightail it along the hillside and meet you there." He turned and coughed. "I'll take the rest of the crew to cut hotline below. Try and buy you some time." He snugged his gloves tight. "I don't know how many times I've had to tell you this. So far you haven't let me down. Don't go and—"

"I know. Don't go and get myself killed."

Warren drew a breath and shook his head. "I should've stayed on the plane." He leaned over the edge and brought his gloves around his mouth. "Tran, Peña, bump up. Rest of Redding crew, I'll tie in with you to cut line below."

Warren disappeared into the twisting smoke. They set off to cut, chop, and scrape away anything flammable in a line between the fire and Silas. Grubbing down to bare mineral soil, their goal would be a firebreak at least a couple feet wide and as long across the hillside as they could get it.

Fighting fire without water. *That* was their M.O.

Silas shouldered his pack, pulled his gloves off, and clicked them onto a carabiner.

Peña climbed onto the outcropping. "All right, boss. What you need?"

Silas reached for a soap dish handhold in the rock. Keeping those guys to baby-sit him made no sense. They'd be wasting time watching him when they could be hiking up the hill. It would take them a lot longer to reach the top, anyway.

"I got this, fellas. Start in on the path, and we'll meet near the repeater."

Tran made his feet beside them. "You sure that's what Warren wanted?"

Silas ignored him. "Keep your HTs on local. If it gets too hot, bump out and cut yourselves a safety zone."

Tran stared up the wall. "What about you?"

"I'll beat the fire up there. When I do, I'll grab the tech and contact you by radio to tie in on the flip side."

Peña wiped a glove under his nose. "All right, then. Let's go, Tran."

Tran stepped backward, spinning his Pulaski handle in hand. "Don't do anything stupid, Silas."

Too late for that.

He found his first toehold and began the ascent.

CHAPTER 02

The smoke thickened.

Visibility reduced to a body length. A sudden, searing pain burned the back of Silas's neck. He swiped at it, knocking a firebrand into the air.

Halfway up the wall the rock face tightened like a bedsheet. The holds shallowed out, forcing him horizontal.

He gritted his teeth. Nothing but a churning gray mass below. He let one hand free and dangled it at his side, shaking loose the joint ache and forearm pump. Erratic winds pressed against him, then shifted and swished in the space between his body and the rock. The smoke curtain beside him drew back, revealing a long vertical fist-width crack.

He worked his way over, gripped one edge of the crevice, and pushed off the far side of it with his other hand, directing his force from the center of it outward. He lodged his feet sideways and opposite of each other, the roughness pressing hard against his insteps. He curled his toes along the rock contours. It was a difficult maneuver without any gear—on the ground he hadn't given much consideration to the weight of his pack, boots, and Pulaski. His arms shook, pain piercing his knuckles. He reached higher up into the crack and formed a fist. The skin on his hand pushed tight against the sides. An anatomical cam. It held his weight enough for him to let loose his other hand and shake it.

Keep moving, Silas. Keep moving.

He pushed on through the punishing next ten feet. Tasking and too slow. Tran and Peña were sure to beat him. What an idiotic choice. What had he been thinking?

His radio chirped. "Kent, Adams."

He gritted his teeth and depressed the transmit button. "Go ahead."

"The fire is about to hit our line. How's progress?"

He lowered his head. His nose ran. He rubbed it on his shoulder and reached up again into the crevice. Deep into it his fingers felt wood.

A root.

He worked his hand around a root that looked to curl down from the cliff top. He yanked hard and it held firm with his grip.

He could do this.

Silas clicked his radio. "More than halfway there."

"Copy that. Don't dally. It's bumping hard now."

Silas worked his way up with one hesitant hand on the root at first, and then as it thickened he quickened his progress by pulling arm over arm, pushing off the granite face with his feet.

The haze overhead turned a dirty brown, charred wood chips flipping through the air. The root network curved, and soon the grass and earth became broad enough to stand on. He hoisted himself up and crawled to his hands and knees away from the edge. Spot fires from the wind flickered in the grass. The air hung heavy with heat.

He slid his bandana over his nose and mouth, untied his boots from his web gear, and shoved his feet inside them. Pulling on his gloves, he squinted through the smoke. About fifty feet away stood the triangular supports of the radio tower.

Silas tromped through scattered bushes. There his feet met

a dirt four-by-four trail. A white Ford truck with a black grill sat unoccupied.

Silas checked the cab.

Nothing.

He scanned the area. "Hello? Can you hear me?"

He tried over his radio.

Still no reply.

A fierce wind descended on the hilltop. Ash and dirt peppered his face. Silas tucked his head and strapped his goggles in place.

Warren's voice came scratchy across the radio. "Redding Jumper Crew bump out to a safety zone. The fire has jumped our line. Repeat, the fire has jumped our line."

Heat itched at his neck. Smoke from the edge swirled and ignited in the air, twisting into a fire whirl. The cyclone furnace set bushes aglow. Choking air pressed down.

Silas scuttled to the tower and braced a hand on a steel support member, coughing and hacking. Light-headed, he wiped ash from his goggles, unable to tell if the ground swirled or just the smoke. He stumbled and twisted to his stomach. He scooped a hole in the dirt and stuck his mouth deep in it to suck cooler, cleaner air.

He had to get oxygen.

Just beyond the tower stood a large metal control box.

Silas army-crawled toward it and scrambled over rocks. He collided with the box and shuffled around to the leeward side.

The wind lessened.

He slumped in the sheltered pocket, gasping. His vision cleared. His mind focused.

And there beside him in the dirt lay a man, facedown and unmoving.

CHAPTER 03

Silas knelt by the tech and tilted open his airway. A slow breath met his cheek. His right leg twisted at unnatural angles.

Silas looked up at their sheltered side of the control box. A Jeep trail ran parallel to them and across to the far side, where it curved toward the encroaching fire. A quick glance back at the truck showed flames licking at its sheet metal roof and snaking along the underbelly.

With three sides of the hilltop engulfed by fire, Silas squatted low and surveyed his last escape option. He worked his way forward in the smoke, feeling with his boots for the far edge of the cliff. Several road widths away, the ground cut off, diving toward a sprawling forest far below. A couple spot fires punked around in the ground cover.

Silas swallowed against a parched throat. Maybe half a hose length down, the smoke thinned and a ledge jutted out from the granite hillside, a platform big enough for two.

He duck-walked back to the radio tech and dropped his fireline pack. The man's chest moved with shallow respirations. Silas threaded out a hundred-foot length of quarter-inch rope from an unzipped pouch. He scurried to the nearest leg of the radio tower, wrapped the rope around it four times, and tied it off. He pulled the rope back to the control box and fought for breath, resisting the urge to retch.

An explosion erupted. A fireball mushroomed above the truck.

No time to waste.

Mucus ran from his nostrils, soaking into his bandana. His lungs tightened. He wrapped the thin rope around the spine of a spare carabiner that he clipped around the belt and shoulder straps of his web gear.

This was about as down and dirty as rappelling got. No eight plate. No rack. The only source of friction to keep him from plummeting down that cliff came from a thin rope wrapped around a thinner piece of composite metal.

Silas crouched by the tech. No time for splints. He took the man's arms and pulled up his torso. From one knee, Silas tucked his shoulder toward the man and worked him into a victim carry. He shifted to a crouch, pushed with his glutes, and rose with the dead weight on top of him, thighs burning. He spread his legs for balance and clipped his last carabiner between his pack harness and the man's belt.

The rope in front of him pulled taut, anchored to a radio tower leg no longer visible. Silas belayed with one hand, keeping the other on the tech's legs.

Hot wind blew against his face. Brilliant flame lengths shot over the control box, rearing like a wild horse. Silas fed the rope through the carabiner until they reached the cliff edge. A heat wave hit the front of him, cooking his fingers through the gloves and stinging his ears. He leaned over the precipice and took one look down the gaping draw.

He pushed off the edge and sailed down the cliff, rope zipping through his gloves, burning his palms.

Silas fought to slow the descent. He angled up hard on the

rope. It twisted and sucked his hand into the carabiner. They bounced to a halt. Silas shouted in pain. His fingers twisted at contorted angles, bearing the weight of them both.

The ledge still lay a few stories below. The figure-eight knot that marked the end of the rope dangled by Silas's feet. They didn't have enough to reach.

Silas winced and grunted. He pulled on the rope to relieve the excruciating confinement of his trapped hand. It gave marginal respite. He blew out a pained breath. His shoulder carrying the tech felt numb. They swayed, the rope creaking.

He had to get the weight off his hand.

He reached back to his pack and pulled from it a length of thinner rope. Holding the remaining end of descent rope between his legs, he used his free hand to tie a Prusik knot onto it with the thinner rope, leaving a dangling stirrup for his boot. With some difficulty, he worked the ball of his foot in and pushed up, immediately relieving the pressure on his hand.

Silas huffed in relief. He worked his hand free and the tangled rope let loose, dropping them a foot lower. The tech listed sideways. Silas grabbed him and wrapped his other leg around the rope for stability.

Now to just get down.

The fire swirled overhead. Increasing smoke rose from beneath. Silas twisted around to get a view of the hill below. Ground cover in the once-serene tree stands now erupted in a coalescing flame front. The bushes would soon ladder up the smaller trees to the evergreen crowns.

Out of the frying pan . . . His shoulder killed. He couldn't hold them on this rope for much longer.

Where were Peña and Tran?

Silas reached for his radio, tucking his chin to bring his chest pack closer to his mouth. The tech slipped again. Silas jerked to catch him.

The smoke below churned black. Heavier fuels. Thicker trees. More heat to come.

They dangled on a spit, the hillside drawing heat like a chimney.

That ledge lay too far below. If he alone dropped, he would likely break his legs or back but might still survive. But that wouldn't matter if the fire overtook him. If the tech dropped while unconscious, it would kill him. There was no way Silas could climb back up with the weight of them both. Besides, the atmosphere up top was untenable.

An orange glow flashed in the smoke below.

His attention turned to a recessed section in the mountainside at the height they dangled. To a body-sized chamber carved in the granite.

The temperature heightened. Fire wicked upward, and the skin on his calves tingled. He glanced again at the hollow.

A tomb to die in.

Using his Prusik-supported foot, he articulated his body to swing the rope. In slow pendulum arcs, he swung closer to the cliff wall. Silas wrapped his arm over the tech and tightened a one-handed grip on the rope. He reached out with his other hand for the edge of the rock recess. The swinging motion stalled, and his extended fingers slipped over pebbled sand at the edge of the opening. They swung out and away. Silas pumped at the far end of the pendulum swing, driving feetfirst this time. He sailed sideways with the tech into the crevice and spread his legs, wedging them from top to bottom. He unclipped his carabiner from the man and dumped him onto the back of the stony surface. Silas's boot tips slipped. He pushed off on the man and swung away.

The smoke chugged harder, blackening the air. Ovenlike temperatures cooked all around him. Tingling turned to stinging.

Silas swung toward the opening. Lacking momentum, only his feet reached the rock. He pushed off hard, arcing backward. At the far end of his swing the smoke engulfed him and the hillside disappeared.

The inertia shifted.

One more chance.

He sailed from the smoke and brought his body horizontal. The rope hit the rock face. He released his grip and landed with a thud inside the hollow.

CHAPTER 04

Lightning flashed on the horizon.

The screen door groaned. Mental note. Another fix-it for Elle to add to her list of home projects. She thought that renting a house near the smokejumper base in Redmond, Oregon, would be better for them than their small apartment down in Bend. The out-of-state owner had said Elle would be responsible for little upkeep. *That was a gross understatement.* She didn't have the time to worry about the creaking board on the porch, the chipping paint on the eaves, etc., etc. Some things would have to stay as they were until . . . Well, some things would just have to stay the way they were.

Wedging between the screen door and front door, Elle fished out her keys. Lightning lit the sliver of sky between the horizon and the clouds. The valley lay cloaked beneath an ominous charcoal hood.

With the humidity and temperatures, those strikes would likely smolder through the evening. By midmorning tomorrow, new smokes would rise up across southeastern Oregon. By afternoon she'd be flying guys over new fires.

Before Elle got the key in the lock, the latch clicked and the door eased open. A flickering television lit the living room. Cecelia glared at Elle from behind her large red-rimmed glasses. She glanced at the wall clock, gave the door a slight push, and turned inside. "There's a plate of pork chops and green beans in the fridge." She snatched up a wineglass from the coffee table and walked through the hall leading to the kitchen.

The fluorescent kitchen light blinked on, stark and white. Elle glanced up the staircase toward Madison's room and set her shoulder bag down on the dining table. Cecelia stood by the sink, downing the last swallow of red wine from her glass. A bottle sat on the countertop, cork protruding, the wine level more than halfway down. Chateau Lafite Rothschild. The '82. Cece and Mark's most expensive wedding present.

Fury blended with pity in Elle's gut. How could she? How responsible was that? Elle's little girl lay asleep upstairs, and there Cecelia was, well on her way to getting drunk. Elle had extended her tolerance far beyond that for any normal baby-sitter.

When Cecelia's smokejumper husband died last year, Elle had fully expected the transition to be difficult for the woman. Mark had been a good man, and his death was a great loss for the Redmond base. Knowing Cecelia to be far from home and steeped in debt, Elle had considered it to be the least she could do to invite her to stay with them. No rent required. Take the time she needed.

But there Cecelia stood with no regard for Maddie's safety, drinking a wedding-present wine worth thousands of dollars.

It was as though Cecelia wanted to make it seem that money wasn't an object for her. That she didn't *need* to stay with Elle because she couldn't afford a place of her own. She wasn't a charity case. And apparently she didn't need to earn her keep by watching Madison while Elle was off flying at unpredictable hours. Cecelia wanted to pretend *she* was doing the favor. *She* was altruistically stepping in to watch Elle's child.

Elle wasn't going to overthink it. Who knew what was going through Cece's mind? "What time did she go to bed?"

Cecelia stared at the cream-colored window drapes above the sink. "Maddie?"

Elle scowled, but she fought the urge to be sarcastic.

Cecelia leaned on the sink. " 'Bout an hour ago."

Dishes sat unwashed in the sink. "You get the chance to clean up after dinner?"

"Couldn't find a dish towel."

Elle exhaled. "Maddie do her chores?"

"What chores?"

"You know I always have her make her bed and pick up her room."

"Not according to her."

"It takes ten minutes. Did you even check?"

"What do you want me to be?" Cecelia turned toward Elle. "A detective? You want me to interrogate your six-year-old?"

"She's five."

"Whatever."

Elle shook her head. "No. Not whatever. This is what I'm talking about, Cece. I trust you with her. I've opened my house to you—"

"Oh, don't give me that. I could find a place anytime I—"

"Then why don't you?" Elle flushed hot. What would she do without her? Who would watch Maddie? Inattentive adult supervision was better than none at all. Wasn't it?

Cecelia tightened her cheeks, then separated her lips. She walked to the bottle of wine and swiped it from the counter.

Elle steadied her breathing. "You could have sold that bottle and paid some of your bills—or helped pay for someone to watch

Maddie for the next *four* months. I've been patient. I've been nonjudgmental. I wanted to give you room since Mark died. You think things haven't been hard for me?"

Cecelia stared at her, only anger in her eyes.

Elle swallowed. "You blame me, don't you? Because I flew him out that day. You think it's my fault."

"I'm leaving."

"Where? You can't drive in your condition."

"I'm going for a walk." Cecelia ambled down the hall, balancing herself off the wall.

The screen door squeaked and slammed.

Elle turned in disgust. Crumbs and dust littered the floor. Her shoulders sank. She'd clean up in the morning. She clicked off the television and climbed the stairs. An amber nightlight illumined the upstairs hallway by the bath. It reflected off a glass-framed photo of herself at four years old, in her father's arms, his old Cessna parked behind them, the familiar *N288* marked on the tail. She touched the edge with her fingertips and walked to Madison's doorway.

Maddie lay sprawled sideways across her bed, wearing her pink fairy pajamas, one sock off. Her wooden dollhouse sat on the circular rug near the foot of her bed, the doll family tucked in for the night. Scattered throughout her room were stuffed animals all covered by some type of blanket—many with dish towels, others with pillowcases or handkerchiefs. From the looks of it, Madison had put them all to bed and then herself.

Elle tiptoed in, avoiding the floorboards she knew to creak. She stroked Madison's straight brown hair, lifted her back to the pillow, and covered her with the comforter. She spoke to her softly and kissed her good-night.

Lightning flashed outside the room window. Elle drew the curtain aside and stared into the blackness.

Thunder drummed in the distance.

She pulled the hair tie from her braided ponytail, brought the braid around her shoulder, and unwove it, watching cloud-to-cloud flashes of electricity.

What was she going to do tomorrow?

The past two years hadn't given Elle much time to make friends in Oregon, not with out-of-state doctor visits every month and the unpredictable hours she kept during fire season. Work and making a home for Madison took all her energy and time. Cecelia's unreliability drove home for Elle just how alone they really were. There was no one she could call to watch Maddie on such short notice.

She certainly couldn't trust Cecelia to care for her. Not the way things were right now. Cece had her own issues that she needed to work through.

No. Tomorrow would have to be a field trip. Go to work with Mom day. With zero sick hours left in Elle's bank, she'd have to find someone to go to the airbase and watch Madison while Elle was in the sky.

It could work.

For the day after that she had already secured leave-without-pay to make Maddie's next appointment at the children's hospital in Oakland. Another specialist who she'd give her daughter's long and mysterious medical history to. She was beginning to lose hope that modern medicine could ever offer a solution. Elle drew the curtain and leaned over to kiss Maddie.

"We'll make it, baby. Don't worry." Thunder boomed. "Each day has enough trouble of its own."

CHAPTER 05

"Do I get to fly in the airplane with you?"

"Not this time, sweetie."

Madison untied the braid in her doll's hair.

Elle glanced back from the driver's seat. "Maddie. Don't do that. You just asked me to braid that for you."

"Rose doesn't need it now."

Elle's sunglasses jiggled by the gearshift. "Why did she need it back at the house, then?"

"That's when she thought she was going to fly a plane."

Elle smiled. "Oh. Is that what girls do when they're going to fly a plane?"

"Yep."

"Why is that?"

"So the wind doesn't blow it all in their faces. Then they couldn't see and might hit a bird."

"Ah. They might hit a bird."

"I saw lots of them yesterday."

"Where? At playgroup?"

"Uh-huh. They were on the picnic tables."

"Oh. What do you think they were doing there?"

"They were just standing around, like me."

Elle slowed to a four-way intersection with a stoplight hanging from a wire. Across the street a cow chewed cud by a fence. The light flicked green.

"Were you all by yourself, Maddie?"

"I always am."

"What do you mean, baby? You have friends who play with you. What about Stacy?"

"She's too scared."

"Scared of what?"

"Of my shakes."

Elle swallowed, saw a turnout, and pulled off the road. She set the brake and shifted in her seat. Madison sat unfazed and even-keel.

"Maddie, a lot of people, a lot of kids, suffer seizures. It doesn't make you scary or weird or anything like that. Okay?"

Madison gave a reassuring smile for her mother. "I know that. But it's okay, Mommy. You don't have to worry."

———

Sharon Weitz, office administrator for the Redmond smoke-jumper base, scurried up to Elle, fingering her glasses and sweating with nervousness—something of a baseline condition for her. "You know I love your little darling. But isn't that against Forest Service policy?"

Elle shook her head. "No, no. Of course not."

Madison sat in the front reception area across from Sharon's desk, her legs dangling from a vinyl-and-chrome chair beside an oak end table. Her dolly sat on the chair next to her, a copy of *People* spread across its fabric legs.

"I'm fairly certain it is, Elle. Outside contracting on government time . . ." Sharon clenched her teeth and raised her eyebrows.

In her time at the Redmond base, Elle had found Sharon to

be incurably accurate and incredibly trustworthy. The perfect counter to Cecelia's neglect.

Elle waved a hand. "You know there's a federal amendment to the Family Leave Act that provides for auxiliary child care while at work under emergent circumstances."

"Oh. I'm not familiar with that." Her eyes tracked side to side. "Wait. . . . You're joshing me, aren't you."

Elle shrugged and smiled.

Sharon looked down at Maddie, who, without any effort, produced the most adorable puppy-eyed stare back. "Goodness. Well, how could I refuse that face? Darling, you've got all your mother's good looks wrapped in a little basket of cuteness."

Elle bit her bottom lip.

Sharon straightened and exhaled. "Elle dear, I'd be honored to have Madison accompany me for the day. Perhaps we can do some stapling and hole punching together. Hmm?"

Madison grinned and tilted her head. She was already under Sharon's spell, and Sharon hers.

Thank you, Lord.

"Though, Elle"—Sharon placed a hand on her arm—"I'm afraid it can only be during work hours. Jack's mother is with us now, and since her stroke she's needed a lot of caretaking in the evenings."

"Of course. I know this isn't ideal. I can't think of anyone else I'd trust her with more today." Elle crouched by Madison. "I should be here for the most part. And you can watch what I do with the airplane, if you'd like."

"Can I talk to the firemen?"

"Absolutely not." Elle flattened a crease in Madison's skirt.

"You know, I do need you to take care of an important job for me."

"What?"

She picked up Maddie's dolly. "Watch over Rose."

Maddie's mouth turned at the side.

"What?"

"I always take care of Rose, Mom."

"Of course you do, baby. If you need anything, don't be afraid to ask Mrs. Weitz, okay?"

Madison nodded and smiled again at Sharon.

Elle picked up Maddie's pink backpack. "There's an activity book in here. In the front pouch I stuffed two DVDs she can watch in the break room. Thanks again."

Sharon took the backpack and stretched a hand toward Elle's little girl. "Miss Madison, would you care to show Rose the special table in the break room where she can have treats?"

Maddie's face lit up at the mention of sweets. She picked up Rose, whispered into her cotton ear, and then took Sharon's hand and smiled. "We would be delighted to."

Sharon wrinkled her nose and led her down the hall, Rose dangling by Maddie's side.

————

A translucent jade cloud cover stretched across the sky. Elle pulled off her sunglasses and glanced at her watch. Quarter to noon. She inspected the Twin Otter's right wing flaps, testing their resistance by hand. The heat of the day already bore down, reflecting off the craft's white paint. According to the situation report, multiple fires were blowing up across Oregon, northern California, and Nevada. Just as she'd thought they would.

It was almost lunchtime. She needed to check in on Maddie, make sure she was eating what Elle had packed and wasn't too bored out of her mind. Knowing her little girl, Elle fully expected the break room to be decorated with paper butterflies and drawings of horses grazing in green pastures.

She'd taken two steps when the base horn sounded, churning like an air-raid siren. She gritted her teeth.

The jumpers had five minutes to gear up. She had a total of fifteen to get them in the air.

Elle yanked on the rope attached to the wheel chocks and climbed into the aircraft. The check on Maddie would have to wait.

Be back soon, girl.

CHAPTER 06

There was a quiet after everything burned.

Silas's arms cramped in the framework position they'd been in for the past two hours. The scorching outside temperatures and the lack of climbing rope gave him little option but to ride out the firestorm, protected by his layered-foil fire shelter tented across the mouth of the crevice. The tech behind him stirred and mumbled.

The shelter fluttered. The fingers on one hand throbbed, and the skin on his hands felt raw, likely from heat conducted through his gloves. His parched throat taunted him. His back and shoulders ached. He peered out the edge of the fire shelter. Heat wafted in. Warm but not intolerable. The hillside looked like a volcanic aftermath, smoke disseminating into the air.

He depressed the button on his radio, repeating a tired transmission. "Redding Jumper Crew, this is Kent. Redding Jumper Crew, how do you copy?"

Silas had no way of knowing if his team had survived the fire's blowup. He tilted his head back.

Something small struck the foil shield. Silas studied the creased dent where it hit. Another struck.

A voice came from below. "Silas? Silas?"

He pulled back the shelter. Warren Adams stood on the rock ledge at the bottom of the cliff, silver fire shelter folded and tucked into his fireline pack. The rest of the crew dotted the hill, standing in the black.

"You all right?"

"I feel like a baked potato."

He sniffed and nodded. "Any sight of the radio tech?"

"I got him. He's right behind me."

Warren's eyes widened. "How is he?"

"Unconscious but breathing. Looks like he took a blow to the head."

Warren folded his arms. "You know . . ." He jutted his chin, restraining a grin. "I might have to write you up for breaking a Watch Out Situation."

"Ah. Which one?"

He held up his palm. "Taking a nap by the fireline."

Silas grinned. Relief and fatigue washed over him.

Warren called down the line to the crew and then turned back to Silas. "Hang tight, buddy. We'll get you down."

———

Elle's pulse whirred like a propeller. The sound of her footsteps echoed down the hall. Through the glass doors at the far end, white sunlight warped along the glossy concrete floor.

She thought of Maddie, head on crossed arms at the break room table, eyes watching *Sleeping Beauty* again for lack of anything else to do. After returning from dropping the load of jumpers down south, Elle had had all of ten minutes to talk to her before being called to a meeting with Base Manager Weathers. Maddie handled the day well, drawing pictures of the same horse pasture through all four seasons. The girl loved snow. She cut out a myriad of snowflakes that now dangled over the microwave and were stuck to the glass of the candy machine.

"I put them over the good candies," she'd said. "So I won't be tempted."

Elle made sure to buy her Skittles. Maddie had a talent for making them last over an hour by sucking on them one at a time.

Elle arrived at the office of Base Manager Weathers and let out a quick breath. She straightened the pleats in her pants, patted her hair for errant strands, and set her palm on the doorknob. Weathers was almost like an uncle to her. He was a good man and had been a good friend of her father's. But she knew budget cuts had run deep this year. There were rumors of more pilot layoffs, and she wasn't immune. But this job was the last thing keeping them afloat.

Elle felt the knob turn under her hand. The door opened inward and she looked up in surprise.

Weathers swung it in, his eyes fixing on Elle over his rectangular reading glasses. "Just the lady I was looking for."

Elle glanced toward the doors at the end of the hall and swallowed. "Hi, Chief."

"Come on in, Elle. Have a seat. Can I get you some coffee?"

She generally avoided the black tar but heard herself say, "Yes. Thank you," as Weathers ushered her toward a chair in front of his desk.

He poured a steaming ceramic cupful. An oily swirl of iridescent colors floated on the surface.

"Folgers." He winked.

Elle brought her lips up in a smile. "Thanks." She tried to use her opposite palm as a saucer, but the bottom of the cup was too hot to touch. She held it with one hand and a finger on the bottom edge.

Weathers sank into his chair, bald head beginning with a brow furrowed in a stadium of lines. He picked up a brass-colored pen and twirled it between his fingers. "All this is turning my hair gray, you know."

Distracted, Elle realized late his attempt at humor.

Weathers tapped his pen on the desk and leaned back, coaxing a squeak from his chair. "Sometimes managers think they are promoted to the position they hold for their own sake, because of how great they are and how much they deserve." He peered out at the runways. "But I know that leadership is about stewardship." He brought a hand up toward a wall map of central Oregon. "I've been entrusted with much."

Elle wanted to shift in her seat but feared spilling the coffee. Weathers was proving difficult to read. If he was going to can her, he might as well get on with it, otherwise she still had to grease the landing gear fittings and recalibrate the meteorological station.

"Chief . . ." Elle held the coffee cup over a legal pad on the edge of his desk. "May I?"

He waved a hand and she set the cup down.

"Believe me, I understand the concept of stewardship. But if you don't mind, could you cut to the chase?" Adrenaline swooshed through her chest. She bit her tongue inside her mouth.

Weathers parted his lips, sat up straight, and removed his glasses. His shoulders began shaking and a grin spread across his cheeks. He shook his head. "Oh dear. Elle. You have that old Westmore orneriness." He wiped an eye.

Her cheeks flushed.

Weathers picked up his glasses. "I always told your father that if he wasn't dropping jumpers he'd be dropping bombs."

She knitted her eyebrows.

"You want to know why you're in here, Captain Westmore?" He leaned back in his chair.

"Of course."

"Don't worry, this has nothing to do with layoffs."

She exhaled.

"It's because you're the best pilot for the job."

Elle cocked her head. "What job?"

Weathers replaced his glasses and gathered a small stack of papers in front of him.

"Chief, you should know—"

He put up a hand. "Let me tell you more about it." He shifted the top page to the bottom. "As you know, we've been getting a lot of lightning lately. The cells have grown bigger and drier by the time they reach the mountains."

Elle had checked the Situation Report yesterday morning. There were several fires reported, but nothing out of the ordinary. With Maddie at the base, she hadn't taken the time to sit down in front of the computer and look at the latest.

Weathers tented his fingers. "Hot dry winds have fanned several remote starts into what is now a raging complex."

"How big?"

"There are already half a dozen fires being measured in terms of square mileage, instead of acreage."

"That's . . . How? The SIT report yesterday only showed a handful of starts."

"You know how it works. You get a bunch of dry brush in steep canyons, mix in powerful, erratic winds with an overactive run of dry lightning cells . . . and overnight those small starts turn into crowning timber fires. They're making a run, Elle. And they're joining together. We, right now, are on the verge of the largest lightning-caused fire complex the Sierra Nevada has seen in over a century."

Elle glanced out the window and back at Weathers. "What part of it?"

He cleared his throat. "The Desolation Wilderness."

Elle stiffened. Hence why she was there. She hadn't flown over that terrain since—

"I know." Weathers nodded. "It hasn't even been two full years."

She stared at her lap.

"Elle, I am certain you know those mountains from the air better than anyone."

"That's one distinction I wish I didn't have."

"You and I, both." He exhaled. "Your father was a great friend. I went to bat when the Forest Service wanted me to call you back from the search. Convinced them to give you more time. I saw to it that you had Jumper 41 and a green light."

He didn't have to remind her. She'd known she was flying on borrowed time in the search for her dad's private plane. When the energy behind the initial search efforts waned—both from volunteer pilots and government-assigned aircraft—she contin-ued the flights. First up on the runway, last in with sunset. There wasn't a square mile of the Desolation Wilderness she hadn't flown over in search of him—for three weeks straight. She didn't stop until it became physically impossible, until the blizzard came. Eight feet of snow in less than a week. Grounding conditions for longer than that. Any evidence that may have existed before then lay hidden beneath a winter of white.

Weathers stood and walked to the windows.

There had been the large funeral. The dress uniforms and fire trucks and everything expected from a line-of-duty death, even though his had been on civilian time. Her dad was much loved across the West.

But she'd never gained closure.

Weathers studied the runways and pocketed his hands. "The entire South Lake Tahoe airport has been converted into an incident command base. It is the depot for fuel trucks, helicopters, tankers, and planes. They've got crews coming in on immediate need from all across the country. They're being sent out on assignment barely five minutes after they check in."

Elle sat back. She had Maddie to think about. "Thank you, Chief, for the update. And for considering me for the assignment. But I've got Maddie here. I can't just up and leave. What about Jared? He's single and unhinged—hitched. I mean unhitched."

Weathers walked back to the desk. "You know Jared is not the right pilot for this. He lacks the hours and the experience. I need someone who can navigate that rugged terrain—a pilot who understands how to fly through unstable alpine air masses. Guys still talk about the way you landed in that narrow meadow on the Black Hills Fire, hugging the treetops the whole way."

She shook her head.

He placed his hands on the desktop. "You know the area like no one else. I need Jared to hold down the fort here. Other pilots across the West have already been called up. Look, it's not an order. I'm asking you. My type-one team has been called up, and I leave for South Lake tonight. I want my best people on this. Why not let the horrible experience of searching for your father get turned around to serve a beneficial goal?"

She felt like an anvil had been laid in her lap. She studied the acoustic tiles on the ceiling.

No. There was no way. She didn't even have child care for Maddie anymore. She brought her shoulders back, composed herself, and looked the chief in the eye. "Thank you again. I appreciate what you did to allow me to search for my dad. But there are circumstances in my life that prevent me from being able to take a long-term assignment away."

He stared at the desk and nodded. "I completely understand."

Elle scooted back her seat. It was settled then. "Great."

"You're referring to Madison—correct?"

"Yes."

"Saw her in the break room earlier. She's getting big." He rubbed his hands together. "I spoke with Sharon a bit about your . . . predicament."

Good old Sharon, as talkative as ever.

"It's a shame you're having trouble with Cecelia. I know having her living with you has been a huge benefit. I put some thought to your circumstance, and I have a proposition for you."

Elle narrowed her eyes. "What is it?"

"Carol and I have been married thirty years. All of our children are out of the house now, but she is a very happy grandmother. Every summer we have our grandchildren come visit us at our vacation cabin on the east shore of Lake Tahoe. I say *us*. But, really, I should say *her*—as I am inevitably committed on a fire right about the time they come up."

Where was he going with this?

"The lower level of the cabin is like its own apartment. The kids use it as a big playroom, mainly."

"What are you proposing?"

"I've spoken with Carol about it. The timing is perfect. She'd be more than happy to watch little Madison—free of charge, of course—along with our two grandchildren for the duration of your stay in South Lake . . . if that's something you'd consider."

Elle had come into this meeting expecting news of more layoffs, and here she was being offered free child care from her boss's wife and a fire assignment in Tahoe. "I don't know what to say. I—"

"There's lodging at the airport, of course. Bunk beds and small rooms. You can always pick up Madison after your on-call shifts and bring her back there. But our downstairs has a small spare bedroom and a full bath. You're more than welcome to stay there for the interim."

It sounded too good to be true. But maybe it was what Elle needed. An answer to prayer. Get out of Oregon and away from the rickety old rental house. And how could she turn down free baby-sitting? She gathered herself together. "So what's the catch?"

He shook his head and smiled. "No catch. But I need you up there by tomorrow night."

Tomorrow? Madison had her appointment with the specialist at the children's hospital in Oakland. They couldn't miss that. How would she find time to drive Maddie to her appointments in the San Francisco Bay Area when she could be looking at a max of twelve hours off at a time on extended fire assignment in Tahoe?

That was it then. Elle stood. "You almost had me there, Chief. Madison has a weekly medical appointment in Oakland.

We can't miss those. Best of luck though in finding a pilot." Elle turned and walked to the door. She set her hand on the knob.

Weathers cleared his throat. "Then fly her there."

Elle froze. "What?"

"You need to log flight time for training hours anyway, right? In fact . . . there's a smokejumper crew in Redding, California, that needs a ride up to the Desolation Complex. I could have you fly to the Redding base tomorrow and take Madison with you. You can fuel up there and then make the quick flight down to Oakland for the appointment. When it's done, you just fly back up to Redding and pick up the jumpers for the trip to South Lake. I can have Carol meet you at the South Lake Tahoe airport with a car. What do you think?"

Elle felt a door swing wide open inside her. She couldn't find a reason to refuse. She and Maddie would be provided for. How could she say no?

She extended her hand toward Weathers with a smile. "All right, then, Chief. You've got yourself a bombardier."

CHAPTER 07

Elle gripped the smooth wood of the steering wheel. Violet washed the horizon—night retreating and the dawn making its entrance. Was she doing the right thing?

Elle had jammed everything she thought they'd need for a month-plus into her '76 convertible MG. Madison slept beside her in her booster car seat, gently snoring with her head back and mouth open. The house looked dark and abandoned, silhouetted by the lone streetlight on the country road. Cecelia was gone. A note on the table had explained she was going to Florida—Miami first—to restart her life and forget the West. To find herself. . . .

Elle couldn't help but think that she'd do nothing but the opposite.

Elle opened the glove box and pulled three CD cases from it. Her favorite groups—Phoenix, Arcade Fire, The Ashes.

There was a pattern there.

She slid the Arcade Fire disc into her player, dialing it in to song seven—"Wake Up."

She dropped the MG into gear and headed for the airfield.

Wind whistled through small gaps in the soft-top. Maddie stirred and yawned with a squeak. She stretched. "Put it on number nine, Mommy."

Elle smiled. She played the disc enough that Maddie had already developed favorites. Pastures and fences flipped by, bowing power lines and telephone cables and lonely shadowed street signs, and Elle had the sensation that she and Madison were actually sitting still and it was the earth moving and rolling beneath them—turning and shifting—and all she had to do was play pretend and turn the wheel slightly left and right, the way actors did in the old movies. Soon they'd touch down in a place she hadn't been to since her father's disappearance.

Elle lifted her insulated mug and sipped English breakfast tea. Herbal dregs mixed with honey. The stretch of cool stratus steel along the horizon lifted, pushed up by a narrow band of molten sunlight.

The car still smelled like her father. A hint of Brut aftershave, not overpowering or odious. She breathed deep.

Thinking about it now, she marveled at how he, her dad, finished raising her on his own. Granted, she had already been fourteen when her mom died of cancer. And she'd pretty much grown up at the McCall Smokejumper Base. She'd had free rein, really, about that little part of Idaho, surrounded by forest and Payette Lake. That little section of the state had been the planet to her. It was all she'd known. So much freedom—swimming in Payette by herself and hiking off and wandering to places she'd never consider letting Maddie, even as a grown-up, go alone.

She loved to fly like her dad, but short of a vague sense that piloting airplanes would somehow fit into her future, she really wasn't sure of what the days ahead would hold. But one thing she knew for sure by the time she'd turned nineteen—and that summer with Silas Kent confirmed it—she never wanted to marry a smokejumper.

Strange, now that she thought about it, that a girl raised with so much independence would "settle down" so early. She'd thought she was making the prudent choice in marrying Seth

Riordan the winter after Silas left. The decision had felt stable, secure. He offered the chance at a family a bit more as it was "supposed to be"—in a house in a suburb, nowhere near a runway, and void of men who launched themselves out of aircraft for a living.

Seth had a business degree and a reliable schedule. Promoted to middle manager of sales at an insurance office, he'd left for work at seven thirty, taken his half-hour lunch break at twelve thirty, and was off at four thirty. She never questioned his monthly "sales" trips that took him away for a week at a time. It was part of the job.

They had a sixteen-hundred-square-foot house with a four-hundred-square-foot lawn in a ten-square-mile linear section of town. Two of their neighbors were retired. The house next door was a rental. She'd had a rainbow sprinkler on a hose in the front yard with patchy wet ground and clumps of crab grass, a JCPenney wedding ring, and a belly newly rounding with their growing child.

It was all impeccably, comfortably, and numbingly safe.

Just what Elle wanted.

Elle drove into the hangar, pulled the key, and set the e-brake. "We're here, baby." The space seemed inordinately large for the MG.

Maddie looked up through the windshield and grinned. "There's the twin otters."

Elle pulled their suitcases from the trunk. "There she is. All ready for us."

Wind rattled the corrugated metal walls. Oversized steel-dome light fixtures buzzed, suspended from steel beams that arched overhead.

Madison shuffled her tennis shoes along the floor, squeaking like a basketball player.

"Maddie, please don't."

"Sorry."

"Here, take your backpack and blanket."

"Do I get to ride in the front seat?"

"Yes. Well, in the cockpit, at least. I'll strap you into the seat behind mine. You'll be my navigator."

"What's a navigator?"

"The girl in charge of where the plane goes."

"But that's your job."

"Well, yes. But you can help me with the map so we know just how to fly down to California to pick up the boys."

———————

Elle hung her headset over the hula girl glued atop the instrument panel.

Silas Kent.

Unbelievable.

How many years had it been? Why did she not know he'd been stationed in northern California?

He still looked more like a surfer than a fireman.

Streaked raindrops from the afternoon's thunder cell stained the plane's narrow windshields. The circle of smokejumpers he stood with on the tarmac joked and laughed.

Yep.

Take away the soot streaks from his face and that cinder-shaded yellow Nomex shirt, and he was still just a shaggy-haired kid, grinning through ash grit, with that same great expanse of ocean in his eyes.

Elle slipped her aviator glasses on.

Last thing I need is another baby-sitting job.

She scooted out of the captain's chair, wincing as ponytail hairs hung up in the headrest. She followed the strands down with her fingers and broke them at the source, a ring of prior casualties already wrapped around the thin chrome support.

Elle tapped the bulkhead and ducked through to the passenger compartment, the smell of oil and woodsmoke mixing with the humid breeze that wafted in as she opened the side door and lowered the steps. Madison was caught up with her dolly imagining.

"Maddie, you want to come down and say hi? We'll be here only a few minutes before leaving for your appointment."

Madison seat-belted her doll into one of the jumper seats. "No thanks, Mom. I need to fly Rose to her appointment first."

Elle felt a welling of sadness and affection for her daughter. She swallowed, thankful her sunglasses were on so Maddie couldn't see. "Well, that sounds good. Just make sure not to really flip any of the switches—just pretend."

"I know, Mommy. I'm not really going to fly her there."

"Oh, I see. Well, that's good. Maybe when you're older— huh, baby?"

"Of course."

Elle grinned and bit her lip. "Of course."

She descended the ladder to the tarmac, knowing from the corner of her eye that she'd caught the attention of Silas, the sandy-haired smiler. She set foot on the runway, took a breath, and steeled herself.

You can't handle this airship, Surfer Boy.

Laughter broke out again in the circle of smokejumpers.

Elle noticed Warren Adams and strolled up to him. "Word is I'm supposed to taxi you up and over yonder. That about right, Mr. Adams?"

Warren grinned with his square, silver-stubbled jaw. "Westmore, what're you doin'?"

Elle brought her palms up at her sides. "Ain't it obvious by now? What about you all?"

He hugged her, heavy with the humid odor of sweat and soot. "Huey dropped us off about five minutes ago. Saw Jumper 41 circling to land and had a feeling it might be you. How's your little girl?"

"Wonderful." Elle pointed to the plane.

"No, no. I meant Madison, not the Twin Otter."

"So did I. She's in there right now."

"No kidding? Taking her to be with you in South Lake?"

"There's a lot to it, actually. But she did most of the flying down here, so it was a nice break. Got myself a good nap in."

Warren chuckled.

Elle ran her hand along her braid. "So how was your jump?"

"Good, good. Growing fire this side of the Sierras. Small in comparison to what's blowing up in the Desolation Wilderness. We were sent in to pull out an injured radio tech."

"Is he going to be okay?"

"He has a pretty gnarly leg fracture and a concussion. But he's alive. Last I heard he's awake now and recovering in the hospital ICU."

Silas cleared his throat.

Warren threw a sideways glance. "Where are my manners? Elle, this here's Silas Kent. A man instrumental in the rescue.

I've been trying to groom him for the next spotter promotion, but some things take easier than others." He winked at Silas.

She extended a hand, all business. "Good to see you again, Kent."

Warren raised his eyebrows. "You two already know each other?"

Silas wrapped his coarse fingers around hers, looked in her eyes, and smiled. "We flew together for a while. But it's been years."

On the far end of the circle, a slouching jumper spat on the tarmac.

Elle took advantage of the distraction and pulled her hand back. "Hey now, McJumper. You going to clean that up off my runway?"

A Hispanic man beside Silas laughed to himself. "She said *Mic*-Jumper."

Warren scratched his jaw. "Been here five minutes and it's already her runway."

She pointed a finger at Warren. "You better believe it."

The spitter straightened, teeth littered with tobacco. "If cleaning that up means I get to fly with you, pretty lady, then absolutely."

Thunder rolled overhead. Rain spat on the tarmac in dime-sized circles.

"All right, boys," Warren said. " 'Nuff of that. Go get showered and fed, and I'll find out if we get the privilege of flying somewhere soon with *Captain* Westmore here, as we will respectfully address her from this point on."

The crew shuffled off.

Warren patted Elle on the shoulder and started toward the

base. "Good to see you again." He threw a glance at Silas. "You coming?"

Silas hesitated, and Warren put up a hand. "Never mind. Don't know why I asked."

"Mommy, can I come down now?" Madison stood in the passenger compartment doorway.

Elle turned. "Not now, baby, we're just going to get fuel and then get right back in the air for your appointment."

She faced Silas and smiled. *Mr. Kent, meet my daughter.*

Silas stood there, a look on his face like he'd seen a host of angels.

Elle breathed out a laugh. "Are you all right?"

He glanced at her, back at the plane, and ran a hand through his hair. "That's your daughter."

Elle bit her lower lip and nodded. "Yeah."

His eyes fell to her left hand.

She shifted her weight. *Let him wonder—he deserves it.*

Returning his attention to her little girl, he whispered, "She's beautiful."

She wiped a raindrop from her forehead. "Thank you."

"Four?"

"Five."

His eyebrows rose. She could see him doing the math in his head.

Yes, Surfer Boy, I got married and pregnant less than six months after you left.

He looked at the ground and blew out a breath. Smiling, teeth white against his ruddy cheeks, he flipped up a pocket flap on his brush shirt. "You know, I actually have something for you."

That she didn't expect. Her voice laced with cynicism. "You brought me something. That's a good one. It's been, what, seven years? You didn't even know you'd see me here."

She spotted the fuel truck coming down the tarmac. Oh, the things she wanted to say to him. She thought of half a dozen beginnings, certain that all of them would devolve into an argument. Okay. She'd humor him. "So, what is it?"

From his shirt pocket Silas produced green sprigs, slightly charred at the tips. "Found this on the hike to the helicopter landing zone." He plucked a leaf, tossed it into his mouth, and handed her the rest.

Elle looked from him to the leaves. She held them to her nose and breathed in. She closed her eyes and smiled. *Mint.* That summer at the beach . . .

Wait.

How'd he do that? What was the matter with her anyway?

She plucked a couple leaves and handed the bouquet back. "Wild mint." She turned and started walking back to the plane. "Thank you." She popped a leaf into her mouth and stuck the other in her pocket.

He trotted up next to her. "It wasn't like I just pocketed it for myself. I'm not lying when I say this—you were the first person I thought of."

Elle raised and lowered her eyebrows. This wasn't going to go anywhere. She turned to the horizon. "Another cold front's coming in."

"It's good to see you again, Elle."

She pasted on a smile. *Be strong.* "It is good to see you. . . . And Warren too."

"Oh. Me and Warren."

"Yes."

"I heard you mention an appointment. . . . Is your girl sick?"

Maddie was off limits. "She . . . no. She has a condition, and they're letting me take her to a specialist in Oakland." The sky turned cobalt and cauliflower. Virga pulled like cotton from boomers in the distance.

He nodded, not taking his eyes off her. She saw in his face something sad, something more . . . grown-up.

His next words surprised her.

"You think that, maybe, you might want some company down to Oakland?"

She froze, dumbfounded, then snapped her jaw shut. She swallowed. There had to be a hundred reasons why this wasn't a good idea. Wind blew hair strands across her eyes. She studied him. *Don't say it. Don't say it.* "Okay."

He smiled and shouldered his fireline pack. "Okay if I bring this along?"

"Yeah." She nodded. "That'd be fine." She eyed him head to toe. "You're a mess. You sure you don't want to—" She nodded toward the airbase, insinuating he should take a shower.

He opened his mouth and glanced back. She could tell he was considering whether she'd leave without him.

That *she* would leave *him* . . .

She smiled at the subtle turning of the tables. She had said he could come along. She wasn't going to furtively slip away. "Go ahead. It'll take me at least fifteen minutes to get the plane refueled and ready to go."

He grinned this time. "I'll be right back."

CHAPTER 08

Silas peeled off his navy blue T-shirt and tossed it on the locker room bench. What was he thinking? He was so impulsive. Asking to fly along with Elle on a whim after walking out on her seven years earlier. Real classy.

Still, was it wrong to want to fly with her? Did he make a bad decision? All he knew was that the moment he saw her, emotions and memories he thought well guarded flooded his mind and heart. Her presence felt like salve for a yearning years suppressed and too often ignored.

A thick cloud of soap-scented steam billowed from the showers. He kicked off his pants and dropped them onto his sweat-and-smoke-saturated clothing pile. His cell phone vibrated on the wooden bench top. Ignoring it, he wrapped a coarse white towel around his waist. The phone vibrated again, working its way toward a precipitous drop onto the tile floor. Warren's number flashed across the screen. Silas stretched his neck and stared into the fog overhead.

Had it been anyone else . . .

The phone buzzed and toppled. Silas snatched it in the air. " 'Sup, Warren?"

"Long time no talk. Catch you in the middle of anything?"

"Almost."

"Just got a call from the Desolation Complex Incident

Command. The IC wants us on the tarmac in South Lake by sundown."

Silas angled his jaw and exhaled. "All right. When are we heading out?"

"Early evening. Captain Westmore has orders to make a quick flight into Oakland. When she returns, we'll load up and make haste."

"About that flight to Oakland. You have any objections to my joining her?"

The line stayed silent for several seconds. "I don't see why not. Just make sure you've got your stuff packed for a long stay in South Lake."

"I will. Thanks. So the IC didn't say anything else?"

"Nothing, though I get the feeling the whole thing is blowing up. I'll let you know as I hear more."

———

Elle exhaled. She honestly didn't know what she was doing. She was a single mom, not a single girl in her early twenties. Sounds of Maddie singing a redundant refrain—"I'm bored, I'm bored, I'm bored"—to the tune of "We're Off to See the Wizard" came from the crew compartment. The fuel truck arrived and connected to Jumper 41.

Her mind trailed off to a little over seven years ago. Claiming it was on a whim, Silas had invited her to ride with him and a couple friends on a nine-plus-hour trip from McCall, Idaho, to Seaside, Oregon. They weren't an item yet. It had just worked out that they both were on three days' leave. It'd be a lot of driving, but he really wanted to camp by the Pacific. She didn't know him very well, but it was the kind of decision a single girl with no ties could make.

She'd stood out on the front walkway of her house before dawn that Friday with a backpack slung over one shoulder and a sleeping bag under her other arm. She heard the sound of his VW bus approaching before she saw it. A long surfboard lay strapped to the top.

Inside, Silas sat behind the wheel. No other passengers. She hopped up in the front seat, said "Morning," and inquired who they were going to pick up next. Silas looked sheepish and admitted that his buddies had bowed out last minute. He totally understood if she decided not to go. She eyed him, searching for any sign of deceit or trickery. Satisfied that none existed, she set her backpack and sleeping bag behind the seat and kicked a foot up on the dash. "Well, I for one," she said, "am glad to have someone else do the flying."

He flashed his ineffable grin, dropped the column shift in gear, and they were off.

Late afternoon in Seaside they bought fresh fruit and a bunch of mint at a farmer's market. She reclined against a warm sand dune by the empty beach parking lot. She peeled an orange, the scent of citrus covering her fingertips, the cool taste of leafy herbs on her tongue. Silas stood in his wetsuit on the frame borders of the bus, dancing to Donovan on the AM radio with the sun behind him, giant and amber and sinking beneath the horizon.

He sang along, " 'Superman or Green Lantern ain't got nothin' on me.' "

She grinned and shook her head.

He pointed to her and started in on the next verse when she

heard the sound of wet rubber squeaking over metal. His eyes flashed big and he tumbled over the side.

Elle held her breath and sat forward.

Silas popped up, sand on his face and shoulder. He boogied into the parking lot like nothing had happened.

She burst into laughter.

He darted forward, a playful look in his eyes. She yelped and twisted to scramble up the dune, her orange dropping and rolling in the sand. He snatched her by the waist, and before she knew it, the earth turned upside down, with her pounding fists on his back like a cavewoman swept off the ground.

"Let me down, you."

"Time to get wet."

"No!" Her voice came out as a scream. She already felt water from his wetsuit soaking through her clothing. She was so not in the mood to be dunked into a fifty-five-degree ocean.

Silas just laughed and spanked her. Elle gritted her teeth. How humiliating. She knew that the more she screamed and kicked the funnier he would think it was. Maybe if she just played like it was no big deal . . . He wouldn't really dunk her in the water. Right?

Elle feigned going unconscious.

"Hey," Silas said. "You still awake back there?"

She opened her eyes lazily. "Hmm? Oh yes. Just relaxing." Maybe her strategy would work.

Silas stopped walking. The sound of the waves crashed louder. He slid her body forward until her toes touched wet sand. She faced him, hands on his arms, his own tight around the small of her back. Frigid seawater rushed over her heels. She stifled a yelp at the icy cold.

"There," he said. "Told you you'd get wet."

She ran her hand along his biceps. His wet, sand-colored hair lay swept across his forehead, long enough to be a bit shaggy but short enough to be irresistibly cute. And those eyes . . . She swallowed and bit her lip. She was smitten. How had this happened? She was a U.S. Forest Service pilot. Could there be anything more old hat than a smokejumper? So why did she quiver like a cup of Jell-O? She traced her fingers over his chest. In the neoprene wetsuit he actually did resemble a lean, chiseled superhero. Just for her.

He glanced at the sunset and then looked into her eyes. "I agree with the song, you know."

"About Green Lantern?"

"About when you've made your mind up, forever to be . . ." He held her gaze for a moment longer, then searched the sand near them. "Here." He knelt and broke off a thin strand of dried kelp.

Elle tented her eyebrows. "Ew."

He smiled. "What do you mean, 'Ew?' Look." He threaded it between his fingers, brushing off the sand. "Fashioned by the sea and purified by the sun."

The water washed around her ankles, the sand burying her toes. The cold was no longer so shocking.

"Let me see your hand."

Elle reached out her right hand.

"Not that one. The left one."

Something fluttered in Elle's breast. She hesitated and lifted her hand. He took the ring finger.

She shook her head. "Uh-uh. That one is reserved."

He raised an eyebrow. "Is it now? For whom?"

"Don't know yet."

"Okay. How about the right, then."

She nodded and offered it.

"This is what I mean." He took the seaweed and tied it around her right ring finger. She looked up from it.

He shuffled backward, dancing. " 'Superman or Green Lantern ain't got nothing on me.' "

———————

Silas returned, cleaned up and wearing a fresh navy blue Redding Smokejumpers T-shirt and a pair of multi-pocketed Forest Service–issue dark green pants. She watched as he greeted Madison at the crew compartment door. Maddie perked up from her doldrums and put on her best ladylike manners. Funny, she never did that with the jumpers back in Oregon.

"Madison, this is Mr. Kent. He's going to be joining us on our flight to Oakland."

Maddie nodded to Silas. "Good to meet you. You can sit in the back."

"Maddie—"

"It's all right." Silas slightly raised a hand and addressed Madison. "You know, I feel right at home in the back."

"That's good. 'Cause my mom needs to fly in front, and I need to read the maps. But if you want, I can bring you stuff."

"Bring me stuff?"

"Yeah. Like when you're on a plane and a lady brings you stuff like soda and cookies."

Silas scratched his chin. "Well, I guess that would make riding in the back less lonely."

Maddie's eyebrows angled and she nodded. "Yeah. I don't

want you to be lonely. It'll be fun. Let me ask my mom if you can sit in the front, too. Mom—"

"Yes, dear. That'd be fine." She put a hand on her arm. "Can you do me a favor and show Mr. Kent the copilot seat in the cockpit?"

"Sure. C'mon, Mr. Kent." Maddie cupped a hand by her mouth and leaned toward him. "But don't flip any switches. My mom gets mad when you touch stuff." They disappeared into the plane.

Elle bit her cheek. What was she doing? She started her walk around the plane, running a hand along the hull. She clasped the diagonal wing support with one hand and stepped around the tire. From the cockpit-door window Madison waved to her, Silas smiling behind her.

She was already regretting saying yes to bringing him along. Like all jumpers, he was a proven risk. A big one. He thrived on the unpredictable, on being unfettered. She had to be honest with herself. What could have really changed with him? The man jumped into fires for a living.

She'd already been burned by him once.

Elle reeled in her emotions. She felt better with a sense of control over the situation. Guard against the charm. She could read stormy skies. And she knew how to navigate unpredictable weather.

This would be a ride along. Little more. They'd perhaps reminisce on old times, smooth over some hurts, but that was that.

Some relationships were beyond redemption.

Elle's voice entered Silas's ears through the headset speakers. "Did you see that lightning flash, Maddie? . . . Maddie? Baby, you're missing it." She let out a quick, humored breath. "She's conked out already."

"Everything is a miracle at this age, unless you're too tired to stay up for it." He gritted his teeth as soon as he said it. Who was he to say something like that? As though he understood what it was like to be a parent. What did he know about things looking like miracles at Maddie's age? Elle must think him such a joke.

Silas looked back at the crew cabin, at the swaying netted webbing, at the chrome D-rings and the bold-typed warning instructions beside the door latch.

Actually, he did know. He remembered. Despite everything.

Elle sighed—soft, relaxed—somehow asking the perfect question, "Do you remember much about being five?"

The San Mateo Home for Boys. The foster homes. He wasn't sure how much of his memories were from being five. But they lingered vividly in his head. "I guess I remember always being me." A subtle hum of static filled the space after his words.

"Is this still a miracle to you?"

"What? The weather?"

"Life. Creation. All of it."

"Absolutely. Maybe that's why it doesn't seem so different. For as long as I can remember, I've always known that there was something more in all this. That the sun and the trees and the wind, the smell and feel of it all, were . . ." He shook his head, searching for words. "I don't know. Evidence of God, I guess. Of His Spirit. That He loved me."

"*Loved?*"

"Yeah."

"Not *loves?*"

Perceptive, that woman. "That's what it says in the Bible, doesn't it? That 'God so *loved* the world . . . ' "

The plane leaned to the right. "There's the children's hospital."

"Where?"

"At our two o'clock."

"I see it."

"I'll radio the tower and get us in the pattern to land."

CHAPTER 09

It was only a cab ride, and Maddie sat beside Elle just the way she had so many other times, lap belted so she didn't need her car seat. Why should one variable make Elle feel so awkward? Silas sat staring out the window, his arm stretched over the top of the backseat, behind Maddie and her. Elle forced herself to keep her face forward, though her eyes couldn't help wandering to the black sparkled shoes on Madison's dangling feet and then to Silas's shirt that accented the subtle angles of his torso.

Green light. They rolled a block. Red light. Shadowed beneath the Tribune building and its giant clock tower in downtown Oakland. The thought she'd been suppressing crept in, like a stray cat slinking through an open door.

This had the feeling of a family.

The corners of his eyes bore the beginnings of wrinkles, a mark of maturity but not yet age. Outwardly he was the image of adult youthfulness. Inwardly . . . What did she see going on? Turbulence, perhaps? She knew a few things about that.

Why did she feel so old?

She was doing all right. Wasn't she? Providing for Madison, doing what single moms do. Making it work.

It had been two years now, and the doctors weren't any closer to finding a solution to Maddie's seizures. They'd eliminated the obvious causes but couldn't figure out why her little girl had suddenly and increasingly fallen victim to flash bolts of electricity firing off in her brain, sending her body into convulsions and drugging her mind into a postictal state until she woke wondering why her tongue was bleeding again.

This was Elle's life now. Flying over fires and driving to doctors.

It was good for Silas to see this, to see the reality of a mother's love and commitment. She didn't want him to have any illusions. She wasn't twenty-two and unfettered. Undoubtedly, he was already squirming in his seat, ready to bail and find something that better suited his capricious fancies.

————

She looked like a five-year-old version of her mother, bouncing on Elle's shoulder with the rhythm of her stride.

How did that woman walk so fast with a sleeping five-year-old in arm? Silas had to skip-jog to keep up with her in the hospital corridor.

Elle flashed an irritated glance at him. "You really don't have to follow us. The cafeteria here is actually pretty good."

"Why don't you let me carry her? She's got to be lighter than my fireline pack."

She let out a quick sigh. "I'm fine, thank you." She turned down an adjoining hallway. Madison's arm dangled like a pendulum.

They approached an intersecting corridor. Silas caught a glimpse of the numbering. Elle hooked left. Silas paused. "Two-eighteen, right?"

Elle turned, and Madison stirred.

"Here," Silas brought out his hands. "Why don't you let me take her?"

Elle stared at him. "It's just down the hall."

"How do you know?"

"I've been here lots of times, Silas. Plenty without any help."

"I thought this was your first visit to this specialist."

She exhaled and readjusted her daughter in her arms. Madison lifted her head. "Mommy. Where are we?"

Winded, she said, "We're going to see a new—"

"A new what, Mommy?"

"Doctor, baby. New doctor."

Elle lowered Madison to the floor. "Here, Maddie. I need you to walk."

"But I'm tired."

"No. This is your job right now."

"I don't want to walk."

Elle strode ahead. Madison planted her feet together in the middle of the hallway. Elle turned, simmering with impatience.

Silas squatted next to Madison. "Hey, Maddie."

She stared at her mom a moment longer, then turned to Silas and smiled. "Can you carry me, Silas?"

He angled his jaw and glanced at Elle. He reached into his pocket. "How about this, Maddie. I'll make you a bet."

"What's a bet?"

"See this quarter?" He held it up.

"Ooh. Can I have it?"

Silas palmed it and shook his head. "Nope."

"Why?"

"You haven't heard the bet yet."

"What is it?"

"I bet that I can make this quarter come out from behind your ear."

She giggled. "No."

"Really."

"Uh-uh."

"Yeah, watch." He motioned with the hand holding the quarter, appearing to transfer it into his opposite fist, which he held up in the air.

Maddie reached for the fist.

"Wait," Silas said. "First our bet. If I can make this quarter appear behind your ear, then you walk the rest of the way."

She pulled at his fingers, trying to pry open his fist. "Let me see it."

"Nope. You have to bet."

"What if I get this quarter out of here?"

"And it doesn't appear behind your ear?"

"Yeah."

"Then, you not only get to keep the quarter, but your mom will carry you the rest of the way to the doctor's office."

At that, Madison smiled in realization and looked up at Elle, who stood with hands on hips.

"So—" Silas held up his fist—"do you bet that I can't make this quarter appear behind your ear?"

"Yes."

"Okay." He let her pry loose his fingers. His palm lay empty.

"Hey!"

"Hey, what?"

"Where is it?"

With the quarter still palmed in his opposite hand, Silas reached behind her ear and produced it in his fingers.

Madison gasped.

Silas took her little hand, turned it palm upward, and

dropped the coin into it. He stood, took her other hand, and coaxed her on.

She stepped forward. "How did you do that? Can I keep it?"

Silas nodded.

She gripped two of his fingers and, with her other hand, played pulling the coin from behind her ear—feigning surprise every time she held it in front of her face. They strolled up to Elle, who looked on with an expression at the same time dumbfounded, grateful, and irritated.

Silas grinned. "Quarter for your thoughts?"

Elle huffed and led the way to a nearby office door. It led to a waiting room, where he sat one vacant seat away from Elle and thumbed through a copy of *Newsweek.* Madison sat opposite a plastic baby on a play rug, telling the doll to watch her fist in the air while pulling the quarter out from behind its ear. Elle sat with back straight and hands pressed between her knees, eyes moving from Madison to the reception desk window. She pulled her cell phone from her purse to check the time. Someone flipped the water cooler tap and filled a paper cup.

A nurse appeared at the exam-room door and called Madison's name. Silas smiled respectfully and watched Elle follow her daughter in.

CHAPTER 10

Bo Mansfield moved as molasses under a southern sun. He liked it that way. When others tuckered out, he kept on grubbing, helmet set low on his brow, riding on the perch of his shoulders that moved with the perspiring rhythm of his Pulaski axe through the duff.

He could contentedly work for hours without speaking. Dialogue aplenty, but little of it aloud. He worked as the cleanup caboose on the crew. He couldn't leave anything living along the line. Just bare mineral soil. Bare mineral soil.

The guys in front could afford to let a root or a patch of grass pass along to the next. But it all stopped with him. And Pendleton had assigned Bo to the back, knowing that he would make sure it ended there.

This time, Spotter Pendleton had them cutting a distinctly indirect path to stop the fire. Bo knew the maps. They were sacrificing a lot of forest land by cutting this far from the main fire. Maybe it was just Pendleton being his overly cautious self. Pendleton was calculating, textbook precise. He checked and rechecked and agonizingly evaluated situations, but he wasn't cowardly. Bo had cut hot line with him many times, choking on woodsmoke thicker than that of a pig roast to save little more than a jackpot of endangered flora. They'd been through enough that he trusted Pendleton.

But Caleb . . .

It was a weird dynamic having Pendleton on the ground

with them for the first time in a long while. Caleb Parson was jumper in charge, and though Pendleton was technically the boss, Caleb carried an unspoken weight of authority with the crew and had, Bo believed, a stronger than normal influence over Pendleton's decisions.

Perhaps that lent some explanation to the indirect line they were cutting. But even so . . .

Bo shook off the thoughts. He was a working man. Let the men in charge make the command decisions. Bo would keep his head down, grubbing at the soil, unceasing in the repetitive motions of clearing the line.

He let his mind fill with the atmosphere of the forest. The scent of woodsmoke and turned earth. The chatter and sing-song of birds. The rat-a-tat-tat of woodpeckers and the skitter of Rodentia. The swirling and changing of the wind and the temperature and the humidity.

His musing reverie was soon interrupted by the rest of the crew.

Richard "Rapunzel" Strothesby, with his fuzzy beard and long braided ponytail stretching to his midback, scraped the earth one tool length in front of Bo. Beyond him worked a sinewy twenty-two-year-old Mississippi native named Jason "Sippi" Fines.

Rapunzel grinned at the dirt. "Sippi, what're you going to do when you get married?"

Sippi spit from a golf-ball-sized chaw in his lip. "Who the— Who went and said anything about getting married?"

Rapunzel shook his head. "That ain't what I asked you."

"And you're not answering *my* question. Ain't nobody here been talking about getting married."

"Sippi, for once, just use your imagination to envision the future."

Sippi ran his tongue under his lip, stopped and looked up at the crown of the trees, and then nodded. "Yep."

"Yep, what?"

"Yep, I see it."

"What do you see?"

"I see a mansion with seventy virgins waving the confederate flag."

Bo almost broke his rhythm. But he'd known these fools too long to let something stupid like that get to him. He knew exactly where the comment was rooted from. Unlike these veritably illiterate members of his crew, Bo's reading interests swathed far and wide. And it was somewhere between *Narrative of the Life of Frederick Douglass, The Writings of St. Francis of Assisi,* and *The Old Man and the Sea* that Rapunzel and Sippi had witnessed him perusing a copy of the Koran. Since then he had been a Muslim to them. If he so much as knelt to lace up his boots, he might as well have been facing Mecca to pray. He wondered how he would've been labeled had they seen him reading *Mein Kampf.*

Let them think what they wanted.

Rapunzel grubbed away in the dirt. "Sippi, you've gone and upstaged my joke already."

"You ain't told no joke."

"It's amusing enough just listening to you."

"If it was about mister and misses Sippi again, you can listen for my fist to come upside your head."

Pendleton glanced down the line. "Bump it up."

He moved down the line with his half-shovel, half-pick combi-tool in hand like a walking stick. "We aren't yet halfway to the ridgeline, and light is waning. Unless you want to dig into your MREs in the dark, I suggest you keep your heads down and your tools in the dirt."

Meals, Ready-to-Eat. Bo had a chicken pasta with marinara sauce sitting in the top of his pack. He could eat it now or in five years, would still taste the same. Couldn't be healthy.

A voice came from farther up the line. "How much line we cutting?"

"Forty chains."

"Total?"

"Forty chains more."

A collective groan let out from the crew. Forty chains meant half a mile. Half a mile of three-foot-wide line cut down to mineral soil. Eight guys dropped from the sky, fighting fire without water. It's what they did. But this indirect route had the feeling of a fool's errand. Why weren't they in the thick of it—felling trees and backburning to halt the fire's progress?

This felt like underutilization. They were the best at what they did. Or at least the stupidest to work so hard for GS-5 pay.

Sometimes Bo wondered.

Like the other guys, Bo didn't have a family of his own. But unlike them, he worked to support his two little sisters in college. Since his dad's death he'd taken something of a fatherly role. With overtime and hazard pay, the job brought home enough to pay a big part of the girls' tuitions. They still had to cover their room and board.

The decision to become a wildland firefighter had saved him years earlier. When at a community job fair Pendleton talked Bo into applying for a seasonal position on his hotshot crew, little did Pendleton know that he had thrown a drowning man a line.

No college degree, between minimum wage jobs, scraping just to keep from being evicted out of his ghetto apartment. He never imagined he'd soon be out in the West, jumping out of planes and scraping through the dirt with a rabble of rednecks.

But he'd learned hard work from his father. Even after his mother left, his dad didn't fall into the bottle or take it out on the kids. He always found a way to get food on the table. Lots of rice. Lots of unglamorous portions of animals boiled twice over. But food for the stomach.

"I can get you through high school," he'd once said. *"Then you gots to be providing for your own self. You understand? You a man, now."*

Not long after that his dad's heart refused to keep working as hard for his own body as he always had for his kids.

At eighteen years old, Bo labored to finish school and make enough money to pay the house rent. Before long they were evicted—sending him to a studio apartment in the projects, his twin sisters, much younger, to their aunt's to finish out school. Bo found himself cannonballed into life, the structure and familiarity of home and family unraveled. It all filtered away through the colander of existence, leaving him alone with a dim and desperate view for the future.

Dust rose and swirled in a cloud by his knees. Sunlight angled through the canopy across the fireline. They'd covered another sixty-six feet. One more chain.

Forty lashes minus one.

CHAPTER 11

Caleb finally found the chance to slip away. To hike without an entourage, using his combi-tool as more of a walking stick than a device to cut line. An hour before dusk, the sun painted a hundred different colors across cumulus thunderheads, mammoth vessels in the sky like nature-wrought warships.

Even though Pendleton had made the jump with them, Caleb was first on the jump list, first out the door, and that made him the jumper in charge. Fact was, he could size up circumstances and situations quicker than Pendleton. And where Pendleton deliberated—an attribute perhaps advantageous behind a desk— while holding a coffee mug and looking at a map, Caleb knew how to act decisively. It gave him an edge, despite the fact he was outranked by Spotter Pendleton. Caleb knew that the balance of respect in the crew swung his way.

While the guys set up a simple camp, he'd used the excuse of needing to put eyes on the greater perimeter of the fire to hike off toward a nearby hill. He palmed his GPS, walking toward the coordinates Chief Shivner had given him behind closed doors.

The crew had grumbled about cutting indirect line so far from the fire. Fortunately, their belief in the ability of the brass to make effective tactical decisions was already cynically skewed. Who were they to argue with Incident Command? Wouldn't be the first time things on the ground appeared much different than they did in the war room.

Shivner had been right about the timing. Mother Nature had in fact provided a huge opening for them. All Caleb had to do was confirm the find and report back.

He drew a deep breath of pine and sweet smoke-tinged air. It was nothing like working the ambulance in San Francisco. He did not miss the blood spills and bleach bottles and exposure reports. The constant drunk calls. He had been an underpaid people-mover, occasionally able to exercise the authority of an emergency-room physician.

Caleb climbed atop a boulder and drew a deep breath. The air held the feel of electricity. Beneath broadening smoke columns, the land beyond rose and flattened with the organic lay of eons. Natural. Without the hand of man shaping it into something concrete and linear and lifeless.

He'd become a paramedic to spite his father. His financial-advising, stock-brokering, disinterested, and uncommunicative father. He didn't regret the day he walked from the overpaid and insultingly low-responsibility brokerage internship he held. Dad wanted his son to follow in his footsteps, and to stay in his shadow as he did so.

Caleb lost himself in paramedicine, forgetting for a time that he had no real intention of pursuing it as a career, until one evening, after scrubbing his forearms with surgical soap to remove the blood of their latest patient, it all returned in one vehement tide. Who had he really spited? Who had he triumphed over?

Vexing one's father was a fickle endeavor.

This—the mountains, the growing firestorm, and the building thunderheads—this held the flavor of freedom. And if Shivner's coordinates were accurate and his story held water, then it would be Caleb's unique portion of poetic justice.

He removed his helmet, letting the wind wick sweat from his brow. He estimated three miles lay between them and the main body of the fire. Cloud-to-cloud flashes of lightning lit off. The sound of thunder followed. About a half mile below his position, a line of thin wispy smoke wove into the air. He glanced at the handheld GPS and then back to the smoke trailing skyward. Not far from his goal.

It was too close to be a spot fire. Could be a single tree struck by lightning. Or . . .

He looked behind him. He wouldn't be missed. Pendleton was no doubt caught up in planning and mapping out their route for tomorrow, trying to figure out why Chief Shivner had told Caleb but not him which direction to cut line.

The sunset faded into the melding hues of dusk. A full moon brimmed on the horizon, but the main fire's mushrooming column threatened to overtake it. He could make it to the wispy smoke source before nightfall, but it was going to be a dark trip back.

Caleb expected the scent of woodsmoke, but not roasting meat.

His stomach tightened. He swallowed a fresh burst of saliva, lifted his canteen and shook it. The water tasted warm and stale.

He drove the handle of his combi-tool into the dirt atop the last rise before the smoke source. With a step he cleared the knoll and peered down upon a tiny but stout log cabin resting about a hundred feet from the bank of the creek. A river-rock chimney rose from one corner, the smoke now dim and hardly visible from it. A dim light flickered inside a small-paned window beside an open front door.

A strange, indistinguishable sound drifted out from it.

Plucking? Caleb leaned his ear. Not just plucking. Twanging. A banjo.

He huffed. *Great.*

Mountain people. He always thought the sound of banjos ought to be the nineteenth Watch Out Situation.

Shivner hadn't said anything about people in the area. Caleb leaned back against a tree and tilted his head. He would've felt safer if it were a spot fire.

The music stopped, followed by the sound of rustling and footsteps.

An old man in overalls stepped out. Wild, straight salt-and-pepper hair fell to his shoulders. He retreated inside and then returned with an oil lantern in one hand and a metal pie tin in the other. He closed the door behind him and set off on a narrow path into the forest.

Right in the direction of the GPS coordinates.

He disappeared into the trees. Caleb cursed. The man's presence could throw their whole plan off.

Caleb shuffled down the knoll toward the cabin and at the bottom leaned over the pathway, staring into the darkening forest. A tiny glow swung in the distance. He clicked on his helmet LED, cupping his hand over it to give just enough light to walk by.

Gnats swarmed. He kept his distance, careful to stay out of earshot. The man moved on target toward Shivner's coordinates. Caleb paused and clicked off his light. Long drops of sweat rolled down his spine. The sounds of the forest intensified. He wondered if he too was being followed. Ahead, the old man's lamplight disappeared. The distinct sound of creaking hinges followed.

He was close.

Another sound. This one like metal rapping on wood.

Caleb inched forward, willing his pupils to adjust to the night. Faint detail materialized. Tree bark. Branches. The moon peeked through the clouds and the tree canopy.

His boot struck a rock. He reached down to feel it and struck his helmet. His hands felt a coarse rock wall. Clicking on his helmet light and funneling it to a pinhead, he saw that he stood in front of an enormous granite boulder, twice his height and five times that in length.

Keeping a hand on the helmet light and another on the boulder, Caleb sidestepped to the edge of the rock face. He clicked off his light and peered around the corner.

A stone's throw away in a small clearing he saw a faint glow shining from a timber-framed entrance to what looked like a mine or a bunker tunneled at a shallow angle into the ground. From it he heard whistling and the sound of small rocks clacking down, one by one.

The full moon disappeared behind the cloud cover. Caleb checked his GPS. He'd arrived at Shivner's coordinates. The opening to the bunker sat recessed between granite boulders on one side and a steep hill on the other. It was situated in such a way that, even with the coordinates, had Caleb not followed the old man's exact route there, he would've likely walked right past the bunker without seeing it, regardless of whether it was night or day.

Caleb fidgeted his fingers on the handle of his combi-tool. The old man had looked unarmed. But that didn't mean he didn't have a firearm inside the bunker or somewhere on his person. Maybe it would be better to wait until daylight. Approach him with the crew before they set out in the morning.

How had Caleb gotten himself in this predicament anyway? He should have known the plan wouldn't go as smoothly as Shivner had presented it. Regardless, he walked forward. Step by step.

The whistling stopped.

Caleb held his breath. Sweat, salty and stinging, rolled into the corner of his eye. He blinked blurry halos. The methodical clacking resumed, the metered sound of rock upon rock, this time accompanied by the old man's voice. Caleb moved closer. Each step in silence. The voice became clearer.

"Twenty-one. Twenty-two . . . Twenty-three? No, no, no. You didn't do it right. Start again."

Caleb heard the sound of small rocks tumbling onto wood. The flickering glow spilled out the entrance onto his pant legs. The lantern-lit room was bordered by wooden wall slats with bare earth in the cracks. Crates labeled *Explosivo* lined a wall. The old man was bent over a small pile of pebbles beside the circular tin in the center of a plank floor. Beside him lay an open wooden chest and a metal pipe railing that guarded something mechanical out of view. Small glinting veins striped through some of the pebbles, perhaps small extractable amounts of gold. Perhaps pyrite. Nothing impressive.

The man arrived to the count of twenty-three again and then rebuked himself and dumped the pebbles onto the floor before proceeding to count them off again.

The scenario repeated numerous times before the old man ended at twenty-three, having counted off to his satisfaction. He poured the contents into an open wood chest. From his vantage point, Caleb couldn't see what else lay inside of it.

The old man looked up at the doorway and Caleb froze. The old man stared out into the darkness, then broke his gaze and walked out of view toward a near corner of the room. Caleb waited, listening to what sounded like boots descending a metal ladder.

Inching toward the threshold, Caleb peeked inside. Sure enough, a ladder descended through the floor on the near wall. An antiquated dumbwaiter pulley system sat inside a square of pipe railing. The large wooden chest, appearing to be over a century old with splintering wood sides bound by iron framework, rested open beside the dumbwaiter. Inside it lay a pile of much larger rocks, all of them glittering with thick veins of unprocessed gold.

He blinked and smiled. *Shivner, you son of a—*

Metal clanked, striking alarm in his chest.

Rusted wheel squeaking followed, moving the pulley system into motion. Caleb shot a glance down the hole and saw the old man walk out of view, headed toward the ladder. Against the basement wall, Caleb noted at least half a dozen wooden chests similar to the one beside him. Boot steps echoed off of metal. Caleb hid himself just outside of the entrance.

He knew from his internship at his father's firm that gold, once processed, could easily bring a thousand bucks per troy ounce—making a single pound of it worth sixteen thousand dollars.

It was a dense and weighty metal. A full chest had to hold at least two hundred pounds of rock. Minus maybe a hundred pounds for extracted ore and that still left a hundred pounds of gold. Multiply that by sixteen thousand . . .

The whispered words left Caleb's lips, "One point six million dollars."

The pulley squeaking stopped. Boots shuffled across the wood planks. The old man muttered something to himself and slammed the chest lid shut. He groaned and Caleb recognized the sound of vertebrae popping. Wood and metal slid along the floor, accompanied by the old man's grunts.

How many of these chests did the old man have in there? How long had he been living out there, searching for gold and adding trivial amounts to this enormous stash?

The man suffered from dementia, no doubt. Caleb had seen it too often in many elderly he responded to on the ambulance. Could even be Alzheimer's. Would the old coot even notice if most of his stash went missing?

Caleb took advantage of the noise the pulley made and stole away. He strode back into the forest path and clicked on his helmet light.

Dementia or not, the man's presence was going to change things.

It could change *everything*.

CHAPTER 12

Jumper 41 rolled along the Redding tarmac, shaking with frequent wind gusts, the sun low in the sky. Having flown more in inclement weather than the other way around, Silas would have felt uneasy if there wasn't any wind. He sat with the crew this time. Madison looked back at him through the cockpit doorway, wearing a microphone headset with earphones half the size of her head. She smiled and waved with her fingers. Silas returned the gesture.

It'd been a quick turnaround after flying back from Oakland. He'd remained in the waiting room the entire time, and from what he gathered, no new revelations had been discovered concerning Madison's seizures. He took the narrow opportunity he had at the Redding base to grab a bite to eat and then loaded his stuff for what he expected would be a several-week stay in the greater South Lake Tahoe wilderness.

The plane took the slow turn onto the main runway, and the propellers spun faster, cutting through the air with the buzzing roar of the engines. The din leveled at high RPMs and the ship moved forward, gaining speed, the white lines of the runway stretching below them. He felt the floor lift and the wheels leave the tarmac. They angled into the sky, mist condensing on the windows and a world of gray soon enveloping them.

The shroud broke into a world of amber and dark blue, the cloud blanket now below them, a translucent white moon hanging full at their three o'clock. The Twin Otter leveled out as rainbows refracted off the double-paned window by Silas's seat.

How much had changed since the first time he heard Elle's voice? He had been back at the Shack—the small satellite airbase in southern Idaho they sometimes worked out of—sewing a small tear in his chute from their last jump. He had a line of items to put to the needle and thread—a brush jacket, a sock, and a new pocket for his gear bag. It was midafternoon, but the oversized ceiling fan and east-facing windows kept the room fairly cool. So perspiration made its way not in bullets but in slow, tiny swathes across his sunbaked skin.

As a group, the jumpers were organized but free. Part of a greater command structure but not under the constant eye of a commander. There were daily tasks and chores, individual assignments. But they each knew what they were responsible for and made it happen. So despite the paramilitary structure overall, they were given a broad scope of freedom in their days, and it wasn't uncommon to find a jumper sharpening his Pulaski in a toolshed, poring over maps of current wildland fire complexes, tracking lightning storms on the Internet, or sitting in the knitting factory hemming up a pair of Nomex pants.

The monotony of the Shack was not oppressive or dull. It was a waiting. A pattern Silas followed without question until the inevitable horn sounded and he found himself fifteen minutes later rumbling down the tarmac en flight to a fire. But until then, the quiet resting potential ruled. Things moved in predictable patterns. Mealtime offered Folgers coffee, 2% milk, Crystal Light lemonade, or filtered water. One saw the same sights, smelled the same smells, and heard the same sounds.

That's why her voice remained in his mind. It carried into the room like sweet iced tea. Amid the mumblings of taciturn men clothed in predictable greens and dark navy blues, in walked a woman wearing a sun-colored summer dress with wavy brown locks tapered off at her neckline.

"Hello. Mind if I take a look at your new puddle jumper out there?" Her simple words sounded like music.

Silas sat, threaded needle in hand, and stared dumbfounded. Finally he said, "Hi."

She grinned and turned her head slightly. "Hello. So . . . yes?"

It didn't dawn on him until then that he hadn't actually processed any of the first words she'd said. He was just stunned at the hearing of them. Silas cleared his throat. "I'm sorry. What was your question again?"

"I asked if you wouldn't mind if I take a quick look at the new plane out there."

He glanced out at the Twin Otter tethered in the sun. "Oh yeah. Sure. Knock yourself out."

"Thanks." She smiled and disappeared through the doorway.

Silas sat for five seconds and then rose, searched for a good place to put down his needle and thread, and followed her.

He moved on instinct, like one follows a mirage in the desert or ambles toward the sight of a fallen UFO. Other priorities clanked onto the back burners of his mind, and finding her fell into first place.

How often does a beautiful young woman just happen to come across the path of a smokejumper marooned at a desert outpost?

The exit to the runway was blinding. He felt for his sunglasses and remembered them resting on the table by his chute. He shielded his eyes by cupping his hands like binoculars. About fifty feet ahead he saw the woman standing beneath a wing of the Twin Otter, examining the flaps. His eyes adjusted to the light as he approached, enabling him to squint with just a hand in the salute position for shading.

"What do you think?"

She glanced up at him, large aviator glasses sitting loosely on her nose. "The door's locked. Do you have keys?"

As a matter of fact he did. Silas looked back at the Shack, wondering what the others would think about him leading a woman into the back of the plane. He unlocked the cabin door, dropped the steps, and offered a hand.

She huffed, grabbed a fistful of dress, and helped herself up. Inside, she stood, sunglasses in hand, and examined the crew compartment. At the time he couldn't figure out what seemed more out of place in the environment—her or the dress. Though from the way she moved around the inside of the aircraft and slid into the pilot's chair with familiar ease, he guessed the dress was the wildcard.

Silas scratched the stubble at his jawline. He glanced around the cockpit, a bit out of his element. He'd never actually sat in the copilot's seat, where Warren always rode as spotter.

He climbed in, examined the dash gauges, and nervously attempted conversation. "So, you fly all the guys to this parking spot?"

She chuckled and shifted in her seat to face him. "I guess you could say that." She extended a hand. "I'm sorry. I thought maybe we'd flown together before. I'm Elle Westmore, jumper pilot out of McCall."

A pilot? "It's . . . a pleasure to meet you." He shook her hand.

"Silas Kent, designated sewing boy. And sometimes they let me jump out of planes."

She ran her fingertips lightly over the panel switches above her.

Silas cleared his throat. "So is that what you normally wear to work?"

"This? Oh no." Then realizing he was joking, she said, "Of course not. A friend of mine got married about twenty miles from here. I heard they were staffing this satellite shack with a new Twin Otter, so I figured I'd stop in on my way home."

"Oh. Well, that's fortunate. I mean, for you, not your friend."

"What's that supposed to mean?"

"Getting hitched. Now she'll never see you anymore. She's gone."

"I'll still see her."

"Sure you will."

"Marriage is not an end-all to friendships."

"That's what all girls think."

"And guys don't?"

"I can't speak for all guys."

"But you can for girls?"

"Touché. So how long you been a pilot?"

She tilted her head back. "For as long as I could see over the dash. My daddy's still a pilot for the Forest Service. I pretty much grew up at McCall."

"You ever feel trapped by that?"

"How so?"

"You know, growing up at the base. Now you fly at the base. You ever feel like you want to escape and get out and see the world?"

"Well, for one, I've seen almost every state in the U.S. from the air and the ground. And two, no. I love flying. Being in the air is the greatest sense of freedom."

Silas nodded. His whole life he'd felt as if he was working his way toward somewhere else. Even as a jumper, especially as a jumper, when packing out a hundred pounds on his shoulders over rough terrain to meet a transport out after spending the last week saving brush-covered hillsides that no one would ever notice if they had burned or not anyway. Smokejumping was hard work, and it could be exciting and rewarding, but he still felt like it was a stop on the path to something else. He just hadn't quite figured out the something else part yet.

"How about you," she said. "How long have you been doing this?"

He waved a hand. "Ah, I'm still a rookie. This is my second season jumping. I worked a few on a hotshot crew, was lucky enough to make foreman my third year."

"Was probably a pay cut to move to jumping." She clenched her teeth. "Sorry. You don't have to answer that. I didn't mean to bring up money."

"No, no. It's all government pay grades. And you're absolutely right. Guys told me if I wanted to jump, I needed to make the choice soon, before financial obligations made it impossible for me to . . . you know, make the jump."

"So you chose this because you love it."

"Yeah. I guess you could say that. It's been good."

"Been?"

"Yeah. I mean. It is. It is good."

"Do you plan to continue in it?"

Her perceptiveness caught him off guard. Had he really revealed that much in a simple sentence?

Looking back to their first meeting, Silas now realized that his demeanor and responses in that conversation had spoken volumes to her about his character and maturity. She was ready to settle down, and he was ready to hop on the first train to anywhere else.

There was so much of Elle and Madison's story he had yet to hear, but he knew trust was not something easily won, and was even more difficult to win back. Especially after the way he had bailed. What right did he have to be a part of her life now? He didn't deserve her. He knew that much.

Rarely in his life had Silas ever felt a sense of *home.* And now that he was with her again, he realized he had been missing that ever since he'd left.

CHAPTER 13

Bo didn't mind the couple extra pounds. Rolling a hammock into his rucksack was the best idea he ever had as a firefighter. After working in the dirt all day, who wanted to sleep in it too? He'd lucked out for the most part, only on rare occasion making a jump into vast sage-covered hills with nothing bigger than bitterbrush to hang his bed on.

Bo rested the paperback he'd been reading on his chest. The boys had each scraped out their own places to bed down. Cleese tended a campfire close enough that Bo still felt the warmth on the outskirts of its illumination. The fire mirrored off Cleese's bald head. His eyes remained shadowed, covered by the ridge of his brow. Monte sat on the edge of his bedroll, gnawing on something from his Meals, Ready-to-Eat package, twisting an end of his handlebar moustache. Between the two of them they'd spoken maybe three full sentences all day. And Bo wasn't one to talk either, leaving an exploitable void for Sippi and Rapunzel and their ridiculous banter.

Caleb Parson walked into camp, rolled out his mat near Bo, and laid everything beside it in perfect order. He stretched out on it, opened a paperback, and traced a finger beneath lines of text. Had Bo not witnessed the man just walk in, he would have thought Caleb had been reading there for some time.

Bo squinted to make out the title of Caleb's book. *The Campbell Prediction System.* Good reading to keep one alive.

"So what's the greater factor in a fire—fuel, weather, or topography?"

Caleb raised his eyebrows. "You've read Campbell?"

Bo nodded.

Caleb turned on his elbow and motioned at the book on Bo's chest. "A little Kerouac, huh?"

Bo held up the cover of *On the Road* and examined it. "Far as I can tell, this is just about a couple white boys learning a little rhythm from they African brothers."

Caleb released a laugh. "Where do you come from, man? I mean, don't take that the wrong way."

"Oh, I see. You figured I could read—you just didn't think I was a reader."

Caleb scratched his head. "I'm pretty much screwed no matter how I answer that one."

"I'm from Philly."

"City of Brotherly Love."

"City of Brothers, at least. Where you from?"

"San Francisco."

"Originally?"

Caleb nodded.

"What made you leave?"

"Couldn't stand the city. I hate concrete and I hate crowds. Came to discover as a medic that I pretty much hate people too."

"You see the worst of folks in that job."

"Yeah. Saw it all over my shirt, my boots . . ." Caleb stared off. "Wasn't like I left a glamorous lifestyle to do this."

"Who you tellin'?"

"Yeah? What were you doing before here?"

"Nothing. Drowning. Met Pendleton at a job fair. But I ain't riding the promotional fast track like your bad self."

Caleb shook his head.

"Come on, now. Pendleton loves you. You his Will Riker."

"Right. So what's that make you—Geordi LaForge?"

Bo kept silent, watching the nervous realization wash over Caleb's face—the expletive-inducing sudden knowledge that he may have just crossed an offending racial line.

He let him squirm for a bit before blowing air through his lips and smirking. "Nah, fool. I'm Lieutenant Worf."

Relief washed across Caleb's face, and he rolled onto his back. He opened the book. "It's none of them, by the way."

Bo raised his eyebrows.

Caleb turned a page. "Fuel, weather, topography." He looked Bo in the eyes. "It's us. Humans. We're the biggest factor."

"What about acts of God?"

"She can do whatever she wants."

"*Pshh.* You able to control the lightning and the wind? You the one that tells the cheatgrass to spring up?"

Caleb huffed. "All I'm saying is if you take man out of the equation, then you pretty much have the problem solved." He lay back and traced his finger under lines of text.

Bo rested his head on the hammock. "You was right."

"About what?"

"You do hate people."

Bo stared into the silhouetted tree canopy, the smell of smoke light and pungent in the breeze. His eyelids hung heavy and his thoughts turned to his little sisters, and then, as always, he was reminded of his brother.

Jamal and he were never close, at least as far as brothers went. They knew each other well, no doubt. But the seven years between them contributed to a chasm they were never able to bridge. Bo would always be the little brother. Perpetually shunned in public by the oldest, yet never ceasing to hold him in high esteem.

He tried to shake the memory, but it seeped in like smoke—toxic, mysterious, and suffocating. He was headed to the Y to swim. But he saw Jamal striding down the street with a few other older boys. And when Jamal ignored Bo's attempts to get his attention, Bo made a game of it. He'd follow them. Like a spy. He'd get intel on what his older brother was up to.

So it became a game of make-believe. And Bo paid little attention to how deep into the barrio he wandered, how far from the already rough streets he lived on into the even darker and dilapidated industrial section of town. The whole way, he darted from alley to alley, from shallow vestibules to the shadows of Dumpsters, keeping Jamal in sight. Cars grew infrequent, pedestrians nonexistent. Bo kept to the opposite side of the street, wondering at times if Jamal had spotted him as he squinted to see between trash cans, shaking his head with an angry expression across his brow.

Good thing Bo had sprayed invisible power on himself. The same kind he used to disappear into a corner of the house when his mother and father would yell and argue. It made him safe. He knew how to be quiet. He knew how to be unseen.

The air was hot but muggy, and the setting sun cast a reddish hue. Jamal and his group turned a street corner, and before Bo could catch up he heard the squeal of car tires and the crashing of metal. The sound replayed in his head. *Pop-pop-pop.* More tires screeching and then the roaring motor of a rust-brown Cadillac blowing through the abandoned intersection.

Bo's hands shook. His disappearing power had worn off. He called out in a whisper, "Jamal?"

His feet led him forward, across the street, to the edge of the building. He pressed his hand against the warm brick, scared to see what lay around the corner.

"Jamal?"

His jaw trembled. He willed himself forward and peeked around the corner.

Two teenage boys lay sprawled on the sidewalk. A dark pool burgeoned beneath them.

————————

A shriek shot out from the forest.

The sound had not come from a recognizable animal. Was not something any of the guys would have made.

Blackness enshrouded Bo, thick in presence, the only light coming from the reddened charcoal remains of the campfire. He steadied his breathing and clicked on his flashlight, squeezing it in his fist by his ear.

The other bedrolls lay empty.

He untied his boots from the foot of the hammock and draped his feet over the side. He slid them on, shooting upward glances, wrapping the laces around and around the back of the boots before tying them off.

He pulled on his helmet and clicked the LED light on the front of it. Lifting his Pulaski away from the tree it leaned on, he held it in a loose grip in front of him and moved with cautious, deliberate steps.

As he left the circle of the campfire embers for the dark of the forest, he heard it again.

Bo swallowed. The hickory handle of his Pulaski felt smooth against his bare palms. His eyes strained to discern shapes. Copper pennies glinted in pairs, hovering over the earth, skittering about and bouncing together before disappearing.

He could smell his building perspiration, evaporating into the cool evening at openings in his shirt.

Voices trailed on the air.

Bo turned his best ear, the left one that was usually opposite of Monte's chainsaw farther up the line.

Conversation.

No intelligible words, but he was able to make out tones. Harsh. Angry. He clicked off his helmet light and palmed his flashlight, leaving only enough illumination for him to see where to take each step. A creek rippled nearby.

He walked for some time, following the traces of sound until the ground in front of him sloped upward. He felt the forest floor, pine needles poking his palm, moist dirt sticking to his skin. The incline felt steep. He'd have to climb on all fours to get up it.

Shouts burst forth.

Bo held his Pulaski at the top of the neck and spun the grubbing end around toward the dirt. He drove it into the earth and pulled himself up and forward. A thin corona emerged at the top of the hill. Discernable words met his ears.

"How's I to know?"

"How could you assume?"

"All y'all is from the devil!"

The third voice was scratchy and high, like a rusted barn-door hinge. Bo crested the hill. The light atop diffused into the air, emerging, he found, from three fusee flares and one oil lantern in a level clearing below. Sippi and Rapunzel stood at the lights' edge by an earthen mound with a timber-framed opening. Caleb, Monte, and Cleese stood in a defensive circle around a wild-eyed old man gripping a double-barreled shotgun.

Bo lay in the dirt and watched the scene below him unfold.

CHAPTER 14

Caleb stretched out his hands. "Easy there, old man."

"Who you calling 'old man'?"

Monte kept still, barely moving his mouth below his moustache. "Let's not anger the fellow, eh, Caleb?"

"I ain't no fool. Y'all have come for it. I knew it'd happen, and here you are."

Caleb shook his head. "You're mistaken. We're just firefighters making our way through this section of the wood. Maybe you noticed, but there's a huge fire making its way toward us right now. It'd be in your best interests to relocate."

He spat. "Convenient, ain't it."

"Look," Monte said, again holding very still. "This here's a misunderstanding. Mr . . . ?"

"Leewood. Zane Leewood."

"Mr. Leewood, have you considered that you just happened upon us as we were trekking along—"

"In the middle of the night? What kind of firefighting you doing right now?"

Monte flashed a glance at Caleb. Beyond him, Cleese stood silent with eyes shadowed, hands at his sides and fingers extended.

"Yes," Caleb said. "We hike at night as well. We have strategic destinations and goals to reach."

"And you just happened to be in this particular draw outside of my gold cache. A likely story."

Cleese kept quiet, taking advantage of the misdirected focus to inch closer to the man.

Caleb shrugged. "I don't know how to convince you otherw—"

"It's 'cause you can't."

Bo tried to make sense of what he was witnessing. A gold cache? Who was this guy? And why did Bo find himself more apt to believe him than Caleb, Monte, or Cleese?

Something scuffled behind him.

Bo twisted on his side to see Pendleton clambering up the hill. "Mansfield, what's going on?"

Bo exhaled. "You tell me."

Pendleton dropped to the dirt where Bo lay and peered into the draw. Zane swiveled in place, training the barrel of the shotgun on each of the three men in turn. They took cautious steps backward. Steps from the others, Sippi and Rapunzel stood still as statues—their mouths shut for once.

Pendleton cursed under his breath and whispered. "You don't know anything about this?"

"No idea."

"That gun loaded?"

As if in response, Zane cocked the shotgun.

Bo swallowed. "I'm guessing that's a yes."

"Mister Leewood"—Monte caught Zane's attention—"please believe us when we say that we just happened upon this place. We don't have any ill intentions."

Cleese crept behind the man.

Monte continued. "Sometimes we have to hike at night to get to a point where we can better fight a fire in the daylight."

Cleese drew closer.

Pendleton rose. "That's it. I'm going down there."

Bo raised his eyebrows. Wasn't his first choice. But he couldn't let Pendleton go down alone.

Pendleton plunged down the hillside. "What's going on?"

Bo scuffled down after him. Caleb took one look at Pendleton and tilted his head skyward. Monte exhaled, his chest deflating like a balloon.

Bo still didn't know what was up, but it was obvious to him that things weren't going according to their plan. The boys were definitely not happy to see the two of them.

Maybe Pendleton thought he was going to help rescue these guys from Zane, that his presence would be much appreciated and in the nick of time. When reactions weren't as such, Bo saw the frustration build in Pendleton's face. Pendleton was a man who thrived on precision and control. As much as Bo appreciated and respected him, he had understood early on that Pendleton's whole identity was wrapped up in being a supervisor.

Pendleton straightened. "Caleb, you're the jumper in charge. Account for this."

Caleb licked his lips and huffed, shaking his head. "Perhaps when Monte is no longer at gunpoint, huh?"

Zane shifted the shotgun barrel toward Pendleton. Bo felt his windpipe tighten. He had faced hairy situations before—fire making a run on his heels, burnt out trees falling beside him—but he'd never felt fear like that. Fire may kill, but it didn't murder.

The old man's jaw quivered. His eyes darted around. "How many of you is there? How many you got out there?"

Pendleton raised his hands. "Listen. I'm the leader of this group. I don't know how all of this came about tonight, but what

I can tell you is that we're out here to fight a large lightning-caused fire that is working its way this direction."

Zane's hands fidgeted on the shotgun, a shaky finger hovering over the trigger. "You're all liars."

Bo had to say something. "Look, sir"—the man turned to him—"I am in the same position. I don't know how this came about. But what can we do to assuage you? What would make you trust us?"

"There ain't nothing you can do. I know what all you all is after."

"Believe me. I'm not after anything. I just think that, if you put the gun down, then we can talk about this. What do you say?"

Whatever it was that Bo said, or however it was that he said it, it resulted in Zane's countenance softening. Zane swallowed, turned the shotgun to the side and began to nod. "I guess there's no harm in—"

Cleese attacked, wrestling him in a bear hug. They struggled and spun, the barrel of the shotgun pointing every which way. Boots scuffled and dirt clouds kicked up.

A blast fired off.

Cleese grabbed the barrel of the gun and elbowed Zane in the face. The man loosened his grip on the weapon. Cleese seized the stock and shoved the man to the dirt.

Zane grunted as he hit the ground. He wheezed and gasped for breath, his face red with veins bulging. He struggled to prop himself on his elbows.

Cleese stood over him and cocked the shotgun.

"No!" Bo shouted, struck by the sight of Pendleton also lying in the dirt, face down.

He skidded to his knees beside him and hovered his hands

above his back, afraid to touch him. A thick burgundy pool soaked the dirt.

Bo's eyes widened. He gripped Pendleton's shoulder and hip and logrolled him onto his back. His shirt wicked through with blood, leaving only thin flame tips of yellow fabric visible. His dust-coated face flopped to the side, mouth hanging open and eyes fixed on the intangible distance.

Like Jamal.

Grief gave way to fury. It boiled in Bo's chest, sent his chin to an uncontrollable quiver. Strength infused his hands, tightening his muscles, focusing the aperture of intent. Eye for an eye. Life for a life.

He stood. Fear splashed over Caleb's face. Monte stepped backward.

Cleese stared at him from the shadow of his brow. "What you going to do, Mansfield?"

Caleb put out a tremulous hand. "Anyone can see that this was a mistake, an accident."

Bo shook his head. *Which one of these fools is going to hit the ground first?* He stepped toward Cleese.

Cleese leveled the shotgun at Bo. "Easy now."

Bo sucked in a breath through his nostrils. His chest heaved and eyes darted from one man to the next.

Caleb took a couple steps closer, emboldened by Cleese. He swaggered like a politician. "This isn't your fault, Bo. And it's not ours either. This is an unfortunate but—"

"What're you all doing down here?"

Caleb swallowed and glanced at Monte. He shook his head and scratched the back of his neck. "I should have told you. I should have let you in earlier. It was always the plan to let you in on the secret. Once I could confirm the find. But, it was . . . better if less people knew."

"You mean everybody but me and Pendleton."

"Right. I know. Wrong choice."

"What'd you find, Caleb? Gold?"

Caleb nodded. "Enough to make it so you and I and every one of us standing here will never have to work again."

"So long as what?"

"So long as we have the cooperation of three folks. Pendleton, who's now a moot point. Yourself. And Zane here." He stretched a hand out to a bare patch of ground where Zane had been lying. "Where's the old man?"

Cleese cursed.

Monte pointed. "There."

Zane ran stiff-legged toward the bushes at the edge of the light. Cleese shouldered the shotgun and fired an echoing blast.

Zane spun and dropped to the ground.

Bo froze, dumbfounded. He blinked, wishing somehow that this was a nightmare and not real. The lavalike anger left him. He felt numb, detached.

Cleese gripped the body of the shotgun and lowered it to his side. Smoke trailed from the barrel tip. He walked over to Zane's body, patted it down, and stood with two new shotgun shells in hand.

He split open the weapon, pulled the two spent cartridges out and inserted the new ones, clacking the barrel back in place. "I'd say we done fixed two of the three issues at hand."

Sippi and Rapunzel drew in closer to the group. Monte fingered his moustache. Caleb came forward from the men and stood in front of Bo.

He spoke quietly. "I didn't ask for this. Nobody wanted it like this. But this old man, he's a vagrant, a delirious loner. I got a tip from someone that this cache was out here, but I didn't know about this man. No one did, Bo. And nobody will. You follow me."

Bo stared at Caleb, catching a glimpse of the old man's body in the dirt beyond. The rest of the crew stood semi-silhouetted behind him.

"Look, I know you and Pendleton were friends. He shouldn't have died. I didn't want that. You didn't want that. But that's a risk out here. Accidents happen. And he died in an accident. All right?" He sought out Bo's eyes, coaxing acceptance.

Bo raised his chin. He didn't have much in the way of options.

Caleb scratched the side of his head. "You know, I'd hate for another accident like that to happen. Wouldn't you?"

Bo nodded reluctantly.

"Good. Then we're on the same page." He turned and stopped. "Hey, how're your sisters, by the way? They're in college, right?"

A sharp pain twisted in Bo's gut. Sheer blackmail. He couldn't let himself look intimidated. The only reason he wasn't dead yet was that they somehow believed he would readily stoop to the level they were at.

Best to play the ruse and let them keep believing that. "They's got they own lives now. I got my own life to look after. All y'all's been holding out on me."

Caleb grinned, then reeled it in. "Let's say this, you take care of us and we'll take care of you." He offered his hand.

Bo eyed it and then gripped it like a vise. Caleb winced.

Bo took a long deep breath. "Let's be sure, then, the both of us keeps our promises."

CHAPTER 15

Elle dipped beneath rusty luminescent clouds that were half smoke, half vapor, diffusing the last of the early evening light. She forced thoughts of Silas to the back of her mind, relegating him there like the rest of his jumper crew strapped into the back. Present conditions warranted all her attention, and she couldn't let their encounter and the emotions it stirred compete for it.

She had expected the jaunt into South Lake Tahoe to be turbulent, but not to the point of losing and regaining over a hundred feet in altitude in the matter of a few seconds. She was thankful she'd remained composed and able to calmly reassure Maddie that sometimes it got bumpy on plane rides, despite the fact that the drop had made even her experienced aviator stomach jump into her throat. Warren, the Redding jumpers' longtime Spotter, sat silent in the copilot's seat, not showing any concern. Elle figured she likely appeared that way to him too and smiled inwardly at his confidence in her abilities. She took pride in getting her crews safely to their drop points. Having Madison on board just ratcheted up the stakes tenfold. She wished she could stretch her hand out into the air and calm the currents for her baby.

The cockpit rattled with another round of turbulence. She glanced over the gauges and adjusted her grip on the yoke. Seventeen active wildland fires in the area of the Sierra Nevada's Desolation Wilderness. California and Nevada resources were tapped, leaving only skeleton crews to remain for anything else that might blow up in the West. According to Weathers, strike teams consisting of five brush engines each and pulled from neighboring states were arriving daily and being sent on immediate need to unattended blazes. No stopping in staging. No getting settled at camp.

She crested a ridgeline, and the lake came into view. White-capped waves reflected the tawny gray underbellies of thunder-heads. The lightning activity at the moment was lower than it had been for most of the trip, giving her a short window to come over the pass and park the Twin Otter at the airport in South Lake.

She'd flown in worse. But not with her daughter.

The plane briefly dipped. Elle held the stick level, glancing at her horizon bulb and the altimeter. Maybe agreeing to this assignment had been a mistake. What was she thinking—leaving Maddie with a complete stranger. Okay, Weathers's wife was not a stranger. And Maddie would have playmates in their grand-children. She'd be safe. It was better than Elle going on unemployment. And almost anything had to be an upgrade from Cecelia.

A pang of guilt twinged inside her. Cece would have to work her own way through her grief. She had to come to terms. She had to let go of the "but why" approach and accept things as they were. Cecelia had married a man who was drawn to jumping into fires. She knew the risks. She knew the possible outcome. What did she expect—for him to be around forever? Elle knew jumpers, and as such knew better.

Lightning struck over the eastern shore. Elle descended, drop-ping altitude to skim close to the lake, not wanting to toy with any unstable air masses above. She glanced back at Maddie. For all the worrying Elle had done, there the child sat, head tilted back with Rose under her arm.

Elle radioed the South Lake Tahoe airport tower for approach and permission to land. They approved her as second in the pattern behind a single engine air tanker that was returning after dropping its small load of fire retardant. She angled the stick and arced around. The heading indicator spun on the instrument panel.

Another flash burst in the sky. The south part of the lake seemed to spout and spatter like hot oil. South shore clouds tore from the sky, and sporadic raindrops tapped on the aircraft hull. The blue-lit runway lights came into view, emitting haloes in the downpour.

These microbursts weren't uncommon at this time of the year. More bark than bite. The little moisture they released would soon be sucked up by dry tinderbox fuels and climbing daytime temperatures.

Her right-wing engine prop skipped and buzzed. She adjusted speed and angle to compensate for the loss of lift and brought her in, slow and easy, until the tires screeched and the flaps came up and the roaring sound of a safe ground landing hummed in her ears.

Right decision or not, they were there, touched down in Tahoe with the world afire.

———

Silas barely took three steps on the tarmac in South Lake Tahoe before Planning Chief Shivner got in his face.

"You're late." He adjusted one of three radios rigged to his chest harness. Sweat beaded between the receding banks of hair atop his tan-skinned head.

"Evening, Chief." Silas shouldered his rucksack and nodded toward Warren. "You might want to talk to the man in charge."

"Adams."

Warren descended from the plane, a grin beaming out from his growing beard. "Yes, sir, Chief. Give me something good, 'cause you know these boys like to fight fire."

Shivner looked sideways at Silas and took Warren by the arm. "Over here."

They strolled to the nose of the aircraft. Warren's expression drew somber.

Silas scratched the back of his neck. The rest of the crew filed out of the plane. Elle walked into the crew compartment and knelt by Maddie. She caught Silas's eye and smiled. Maddie waved with her fingers. Silas returned the gesture.

Warren returned. "Sounds like things in the last twelve hours have pretty much gone to—"

"Pretty much is an understatement." Shivner waddled past with a limp and waved them along. "Talk on the way, gentlemen." The edges of his yellow Nomex shirt stretched around the pear-shaped arc of his belly. "The next operational period is set to start at twenty hundred hours. You'll both be there."

Both?

Warren nodded. "Absolutely."

Shivner hadn't phrased it as a question. He paused, already winded. "All right. I'll give you the opportunity to talk, then."

"Thanks, Chief."

Shivner glanced at Silas and plodded ahead.

Warren brought both hands behind his head and blew out a breath. "We lost a guy today, Silas."

His gut dropped. "What? Who?"

"Pendleton."

"The spotter?"

Warren nodded.

"Plane go down?"

"He was on the ground."

"Why wasn't he with his plane?"

"I didn't stay with the plane when we went after the radio tech."

"That was different. We had a rescue mission. Out here—"

"You know how it is—if another qualified spotter is available, then sometimes we'll jump with the crew. Fact is, with all these fires and resources stretched thin, Command has assigned one incident spotter to coordinate all the jumper crews. It frees up another man on the ground for every crew."

Silas took a deep breath. "What happened?"

"The details are still sketchy. Sounds like the winds changed and the fire blew up. The crew tried to outrun it with their fire shelters deployed on their backs to reflect the heat. Pendleton was the last one, making sure he had his whole crew out. The fire overtook him."

"Others get burned?"

"Not that I've heard."

How does the head of a jumper crew get killed and none of the others get so much as a burn? Silas would drag Warren's body through hell if he had to.

Ahead, Shivner turned and glanced at his wristwatch.

Warren motioned. "Let's go."

CHAPTER 16

The command room occupied a portion of the South Lake Tahoe aircraft control tower. Can lights illuminated an otherwise darkened room, casting warm cones over a large topographic map spread across a drafting table. A makeshift work area of collapsible tables supported a network of laptops and printers and a conflux of wires snaking to and from power strips and Internet routers. A muffled din of radio traffic and phone conversations filled the air. Elevated voices emitted from a circle of men standing around the map.

"We're getting lit up like a lab on a shock collar."

"Hanes Index has topped out at six for two straight weeks now. When are we going to realize that what we're doing isn't en—"

The conversation broke as Shivner approached. The circle split to accommodate them. Silas recognized the incident commander as Chief Weathers from the Redmond, Oregon base. Weathers headed up the most respected type-one incident management team in the nation. If these guys couldn't manage this thing . . .

Weathers acknowledged Shivner. "Welcome back. I assume these two have been briefed."

"Briefly," Shivner said, drawing scattered chuckles.

Weathers glanced at Warren. "Adams, good to have you

here." He turned to Silas. "Mr. Kent, I assume you know what a battlefield promotion is?"

Silas shifted the rucksack on his shoulder. "Yes, sir."

"Warren tells me that he's been grooming you as his replacement. Problem is, the old goat ain't bound to quit anytime soon."

Silas let a smile escape.

Weathers ran his fingers over the topo map and exhaled. "Before today, I'd never lost a man under my command. I, my team, we've been here all of twenty-two hours. We were tossed a bag of hot potatoes and then got dumped on with a truckload. It is unfortunate that your elevation in rank has to come about this way. Pendleton was a good man, and in the proper time his body will be recovered and he'll get the kind of burial he deserves. There isn't a guy here whose heart doesn't feel like a ton of bricks. But right now we have the potential for the largest lightning-caused fire complex the Sierra Nevada has seen in over a century, and there is an immediate need for a spotter. I'd like you to be the one to head up Pendleton's jumper crew. I'm sure you're aware that we have an incident spotter assigned, so you'd be acting primarily on the ground as their jumper in charge."

Silas shifted his weight. *Why me?* "Isn't . . . I mean, thank you for the acknowledgment, Chief. But would it perhaps be better if a jumper from Pendleton's own crew served in that role?"

Weathers scratched an eyebrow and glanced at a man with a moustache and navy blue ball cap standing at the edge of the light shadow. Weathers seemed to choose his words with care. "You'll have Caleb Parson to draw information and history from. He's the senior member of their crew."

"Forgive me, Chief. But why not designate him as the new spotter?"

"Call it a hunch, but I suspect that, after the loss of Pendleton, most of those guys are wound a little tight right now. We need someone out there with a clear head. Someone less encumbered. Caleb's a good fireman. And under ordinary circumstances we'd have that whole crew off on administrative leave and assigned to a critical-incident stress management team. But we need the feet on the ground, and I'm going with my gut on this. I need someone who can act decisively and adapt to rapidly changing circumstances. Can I count on you to do that?"

Silas eyed the men in the circle, catching Warren's eye last. He set his chin and straightened. "Yes, sir, Chief."

"Very good. Now come in closer here to see what we're dealing with."

Silas set his rucksack on the floor and propped his hands on the table's edge. Red borders were drawn around a vast amoeba-shaped area. Smaller independent cells hovered in close proximity to the large mass, appearing in jeopardy of being absorbed by it.

"As you can see, the fires are burning together, though there are still a myriad of spots and isolated strikes. Several thirty-to-forty acre fires are presently burning unattended. The main fire has been drawing most of them into a massive timber fire burning all the way to the crown tips of these trees. At present, the complex is zero percent contained."

A bearded man with a clipboard waved. "Rocklin, fire behavior analyst. Activity has been difficult to predict. Erratic changes have been the only reliable occurrence. Long story short, the weather largely depends on where you're standing."

Silas stared at the map and nodded. "What's the LAL at?"

"Lightning activity level is high and dry at four, fuel moistures at record lows, though we did get a little unexpected precipitation in the basin this afternoon."

Ball Cap shook his head. "Just enough to stir it all up even more with the downdrafts."

Rocklin shrugged. "Pretty much."

Weathers studied the fire perimeter. "The primary issue is that the fronts are expanding in multiple directions faster than we can get equipment to keep up with them. Last numbers put the main fire at upwards of thirty thousand acres. We expect that to double in the next two days."

"How many strike teams did you order up?"

"Oh, I ordered plenty. There ain't any coming quick enough, though. Closest thing we've got coming is a couple type-one hand crews from Montana and three brush rigs from Florida."

"Florida?"

Shivner edged into the light. "Last year's budget cuts went deep. Everybody's feeling it. But guess what? Mother Nature don't—"

"We do have a hand crew that just arrived in staging. Otherwise, nothing." Weathers shook his head. "I've never seen it like this."

Ball Cap folded his arms. "We got guys who've been sleeping in the dirt on other fires for twenty-one days straight already, and then they get sent straight here with no sign of letup."

Silas exhaled. "So, what's the plan?"

Shivner pointed to the lower left section of the map. "For now we are obviously on the defensive. We've got rigs at five-mile intervals defending the populated perimeter, trying to keep this thing from running through the houses. Due to the fire's relatively remote location, we've only lost a dozen structures so far. Right now the wind is pushing it westward and back into the wilderness. That's the good news."

Warren folded his arms. "Five-mile intervals?"

"It's the closest we could get the engines and still cover all the area. Eventually the eastern and northern fronts of this fire will threaten just about every neighborhood from South Lake to the North Shore."

Rocklin set his clipboard on the table. "Lack of resources is only the beginning. Even if we had more guys, the fire is . . ." He brought his hands up over the large red shaded area on the map. "It's growing a huge anvil head out of the smoke column. Enormous. By this time tomorrow it'll be making its own weather."

Weathers nodded. "Leaving us a short window."

Silas raised his eyebrows. "A short window for what?"

Shivner stretched his hand out over the map and turned to Silas. "Anything we want to fly over this terrain will have to do so by fourteen-hundred hours tomorrow afternoon. That's our visibility window."

"What happens after two o'clock?"

"Beyond that time frame, all of this"—Rocklin circled a finger around an area twice the size of the fire perimeter—"will be impassable due to smoke, lightning, and erratic high winds."

They wanted more jumper crews in there now, while they still could get in. Once on the ground, they'd be on their own for a bit. "How long will my crew be without a means to fly out?"

"Three days." Weathers pocketed his hands. "We might be able to get a helicopter to you in two. That's a best guess. Conditions are too unpredictable. It will be bad. We're just not sure to what extent."

Great. All Silas had to do was leave his mentor and trusted

crew, join up with guys he'd never trained with or fought fire with who just suffered the loss of their spotter, fill a leadership role he'd never fully performed on his own before, and do all that without the possibility of reprieve or rescue from the outside world should things go bad, which they were most certainly predicted to do.

He cracked his knuckles. "All right, then. Sounds like the kind of thing I signed up for."

Weathers smiled at Warren. "Very good. Captain Westmore will fly you and your new crew in first thing tomorrow. Warren, she'll fly your crew in as soon as she returns from that drop." Weathers looked over Silas's shoulder. "Elle, hello. Good to have you here."

Elle stepped into the light beside Silas, catching his eye. "Nowhere else I'd rather be, Chief."

"Gentlemen, I'm sure you don't need me to introduce Captain Westmore. Many of you were part of the rescue effort to find her father a couple years back. She knows this terrain better than any of us."

Elle produced a smile, folded her arms, and looked at the map. "You looking to do a drop along the northern edge?"

Weathers leaned over the map. "Somewhere in that radius. If we can corral the front early, we should be able to direct it away from structures and keep it in the wilderness. Warren's crew will be dropped on the southern flank, Silas and his crew to the north."

"If I remember right"—she traced along the topographic lines—"there's a number of small meadows on the way, and there's a lake up . . . here." She spread her fingers like a compass, leaving the middle one on the small body of water and landing the index on a blank square inch devoid of geographic changes. "And an appropriately larger landing zone for the north end jumpers here."

Weathers nodded. "At this point, Kent, I recommend you grab some chow. See if you can tie in with your new crew, and then get rested up."

"Copy that, Chief." Silas picked up his rucksack. He looked to Elle, but she kept her eyes fixed on the map. He turned and worked his way across the room.

Warren walked with him in the shadows. Conversation resumed around the planning table behind them. Warren spoke in a low voice. "You know she really is the best. If anyone can get you in there safely it's her."

"I don't doubt it."

"You seem concerned."

"Do I?" They walked on toward the exit door. "I just don't like leaving our crew."

"I know. It wasn't my plan to give you the responsibility this soon. Believe me. But, Silas . . . ?"

"Yeah."

"You can do this. I wouldn't recommend anyone else more highly for the job."

"Okay. Thank you."

"So, how was the flight?"

"What do you mean? You were on the same—"

"No, down to Oakland. What's the history with you two anyway?"

"Elle? Oh, we dated for a summer."

"So *she's* the one." He gave a knowing nod.

"What do you mean?"

"She's the one you left in McCall. The one that had your insides all tangled up in Alaska."

"It was a long time ago."

"Before her little girl."

"What happened there anyway? Is the father still in the picture?"

"You don't know?"

"It didn't come up. Like I said, it's been a while."

Silas regretted asking. He didn't need more of a guilt trip. He had a world of other things to focus on.

Warren cleared his throat. "My info is secondhand and kind of old. I used to fly with her father at McCall's, and we kept in touch. Great pilot. Didn't have much in the way of kind words to say about her ex-husband though."

"So she's divorced?"

"No, actually."

"What then . . . ? Widowed?"

"Not that either. The marriage contract was nullified."

"Nullified? Why?"

"Turned out the guy was already married. Had a family in Boise under a different name. Closet polygamist, I guess."

"How did she find out?"

"Somehow it came out on the day their daughter was born. He told her he was leaving, right there in the hospital. She filed for nullification."

Silas blew out a breath and ran his hand through his hair. "They couldn't have been married long."

"Maybe a year." Warren studied him. "What happened between you two that summer?"

Silas stopped beneath the glowing exit sign and rested his hand on the door handle. "We fell in love."

CHAPTER 17

Warren left to tie in with their crew. Well, Warren's crew, at least. Silas strolled down the hall, his heart heavier than his rucksack. He couldn't shake a sudden weighted and gaping sense of loneliness. Was it just nerves at leaving his old team? The prospect of jumping into a big complex with guys he'd never met? Or perhaps it had more to do with seeing Elle again, with reopening wounds he'd fought hard to ignore.

He knew how to do the spotter job. In the air he would scout the fire, find the best landing zone for the jump, and send off his crew members each in turn. Once they were down he'd coordinate communications for the paracargo drop. He could do it all. Just like Warren. Instead of returning with the pilot and continuing as a liaison officer at the base, though, he'd make the jump too and be back in his element as part of a team on the ground.

A slim man about his age walked up to him in the corridor. He had short brown hair like leaning spikes, eyes tinged red at the corners, and a face colored by the sun. "You're the new spotter, right?"

Had to be a member of his new crew. Silas extended his hand with a respectful smile. "Silas Kent."

He shook. "Caleb Parson. I just learned that we'd been reassigned a spotter and are to head out again tomorrow. You've been briefed on the whole situation, I imagine."

"It's a blow to all of us, but I can't imagine how it must be for you and your crew. You have my sincere condolences."

Caleb nodded and looked aside.

Silas scratched his head. "Is there anything I can do to help take the load off?"

"No, thank you. We're good. I'm just surprised they're sending us out again."

"If it's too soon, I can see what I can—"

"No, no. It's better this way. Keeps us from sitting around and stewing on everything. You know?"

"Sure. Yeah. This whole complex is unlike anything I've ever seen."

"Pile that on top of the budget cuts. More work for everyone. Must be the call of the wild that keeps us coming back, huh?"

"Jack London."

"You like to read?"

"When I'm not launching myself out of things."

"Yeah, it's hard to see the words through your face mask."

Silas smiled. "And the wind . . . hard to keep your page."

Caleb nodded to him. "You planning on staying with the plane?"

"No. I'll make the jump. They've assigned an incident spotter to coordinate for all the crews." *He should know that.* Perhaps he was just testing his new leader's resolve.

Silas adjusted his rucksack. "Look, you can count on me to be your eyes and ears here at Command staff meetings before we take off tomorrow. Just let me know if you need anything."

Caleb ran the back of his hand beneath his nose and nodded. "All right."

Silas cleared his throat. "So, what did you do before getting into wildland?"

"I was a medic. In San Francisco."

"No kidding. I kind of grew up a little south of there."

He raised and lowered his eyebrows. "Yep, nearly didn't make it out of that trap."

"No love for the city?"

"It's either that or for people." Caleb shrugged. "I got tired of the work. Tired of working codes in the middle of the night when you know full well the guy is dead. You know what I mean?"

"I can imagine. But my EMS experience is pretty limited."

"It's in the eyes. You can always tell they're gone from the eyes. It's like you can see when their soul has left them."

He held Caleb's gaze. "Well, hey, like I said, if you need anything let me know. I'll do the best I can to be an advocate for the team."

Caleb pulled an arm across his chest to stretch. "Sounds good. I'm pretty sure each of us will need a new fire shelter. And we're low on MREs."

"Got it." Silas pulled a notepaper and pen from his shirt pocket. He jotted down, *MREs* and *Shelters.* "Hey, when things cool down, we'll make sure Pendleton gets a proper funeral procession and service. Give guys a chance to pay the proper respects."

"Sounds like you have a plan, Mr. Kent."

"Please, it's Silas."

Caleb flashed a quick smile and brought out his hand to shake. "I think we'll get along just fine."

Silas strolled onto the tarmac, the sky the color of sliced grapefruit. A fresh and erratic wind lifted heat from under his arms, wicking the sweat from the bridge of his nose. The smell of fire hung in the air like the ominous cloud bank over the nearby hills.

Elle had finished securing the plane in the hangar for the night. Silas watched her kneel down to kiss Maddie. An older woman standing next to them took Maddie's hand and led her away. Maddie clutched a bulging backpack with a doll's upper torso sticking out between the top zippers. She walked backwards, staring at her mother and stretching a hand out for her. Elle waved and nodded and smiled, aviators atop her hair.

Elle.

Compared to her, fire was easy.

Predictable. Impersonal. Silas could watch a fire and see the course of the land and the laddering of the fuels and their moisture content and know what the fire would do. How it would suck wind into canyons like a chimney and puff the smoke out like an old man with a pipe.

Silas understood fire. He knew it like one knows when it's about to rain.

But Westmore . . .

She could navigate erratic air as well as anyone Silas had flown with. Some pilots handled the aircraft with impersonal calculation, executing a succession of algorithmic steps with geometric and mechanical precision. The job got accomplished. The plane took off and made its drops safely. And at the end of the workday the plane was chocked and tied down for the night in the cold dank recesses of a hangar or lined up along the edge of the tarmac.

But for Elle, the plane was like an extension of herself. Its movements became as fluid as her walking, like a dancer knows how to control a hundred different muscles in the course of her movements. Elle flew with the elements. She became one of them, at home in the sky.

Silas only felt at home falling from it.

He pocketed his hands and strolled out to her. Her eyes stayed fixed on Maddie. He stopped beside her and waited until her little girl disappeared from view. "Grandmother?"

Elle seemed to just notice him. "Hey. No. Carol Weathers."

"IC Weathers's wife?"

She nodded then brought a hand to the bridge of her nose.

Silas cocked his head. "You going to be okay?"

She took a deep breath. "Yeah. I'm fine. Just emotional. She'll be fine. They have two grandchildren for her to play with. She'll be fine."

"Of course. She'll be in good hands." What did he know about it? Silas kicked a pebble across the blacktop. "You know, they've got dinner fired up. You feel like grabbing a bite?"

She pulled her glasses off her head, careful to thread them out from tight strands of hair.

"Sure. Maybe that's what I need."

CHAPTER 18

Logistics had converted an old airport restaurant into the fire-camp mess hall. A twenty-person hotshot crew filed along the buffet, faces soot streaked and dirt lined. Silas learned that they had just arrived, coming off the radio tower fire. Elle found a place at the back of the line and kept quiet for the most part.

Ceiling fans waved, circulating air conditioning just cool enough to take off the heat's edge. The last slivers of sunlight glinted off windows facing the runway.

"You know . . ." Silas started. "You've done well."

Elle folded her arms, listening.

Silas glanced at the tiled floor. "I mean, Maddie's great. You've done a wonderful job. It must be tremendously difficult—trying to work a job like this and build a home."

"What do you know about building a home?"

Ouch. "I know. Right? I guess I'm saying that I just imagine it's got to be a difficult thing."

"You don't have to feel guilty or responsible."

"Right. I mean, I don't." He exhaled and looked away. "I don't even know what I'm trying to say."

"Don't stress yourself out about it, all right? It's not your concern. Maddie and I have our life, and you're free. Just like you always wanted." She stepped forward with the line.

"That's not what I wanted." His voice came out louder than he intended, drawing curious glances from the firefighters in front of them. He lowered it. "I mean, look at you. Here you are telling me it's not my concern and you're doing it with a guilt trip."

"You call this a guilt trip? Oh, you haven't even seen a guilt trip. You want one of those? How about you taking me on a ride in a car called 'I love you and want to always be with you' and then bailing out before even the next fire season comes around? What kind of guy says he wants to be with a woman for the rest of his life and then takes an E-ticket ride to Alaska first chance he gets?"

They had an audience now. Silas's cheeks flushed. Amusement lit faces in the hotshot crew.

He snapped at them. "Like you guys never got this talk before."

The firemen averted their gazes, clearing throats, scratching heads, and studying ceiling tiles. The firefighter next in line for the buffet turned and picked up a tray.

Elle followed suit, her voice still elevated. "You know how many cocky bad-boy smokejumpers I pick up and launch into the wild every summer?"

He knew her question was rhetorical. He had to just stand and take it.

"Of course you don't. You know why? Because you think you are the crème de la crème. You can't fathom that there could possibly be more just like you. But you know what? There is. And you know what else? They're all the same crop of corn again and again, every summer." She ladled soup into a bowl on her tray. Her voice quieted. "By the end of fall they're gone."

Silas saw hurt in her anger. And hurt wasn't hardness, and that meant hope. Hope for what? He didn't know.

He went with his gut. "I know what you want."

"Do you now?"

"Yes. It's simple."

She spun to face him, her expression giving him ten seconds to explain himself.

He grinned. "You want to change me."

She huffed. "Of course." She moved down the line. "You think it is about you. You know what, Silas? As a pilot I need to intimately understand physics. To the untrained eye, it seems like I'm defying gravity every time I leave the ground. But I'm not. I'm using lift and aerodynamics and speed." She picked up a pair of stainless steel tongs at the salad bowl and pointed them at him. "In other words, I don't deal in impossibilities."

"So you *have* considered trying to change me."

"*You* are impossible."

"Since we're on the subject of impossible . . . How about eight guys stopping a thousand-acre fire with no water, just hand tools and chain saws? Sounds impossible, doesn't it?"

She shook her head. "Are you really going to play the Butte Fire card again?"

"Worked well the first time."

She glanced at him sideways, a hint of gentleness in her expression. "The Wing Stop?"

The buffalo-chicken wing joint at McCall's air base. The second time they met. But she had not recognized him then from their first encounter at the Shack—a blow to his ego.

She squinted and smirked. "Probably not the first time you used that line."

Admittedly, Silas had in the past found it quite effective to open up conversations with attractive women by saying, "Who would have thought a thousand-acre fire could be stopped with only eight guys and no water?"

Most acted impressed. Not Elle. She had just stared at him— appearing more amused than anything. But he could tell she liked the fact he was trying. He had won her over with his show of confidence.

She had won him over by seeing right through it.

———

Elle sipped her iced tea. Sweet tea with lemon. She fought to keep from smiling too much. How did he do that, anyway? She'd gone from being so mad at him when they stood in line— incensed, really. And here she was, twenty minutes later, giggling like a giddy college girl.

Her ability to hide her feelings was slipping from her grasp. She was exhausted. Overwhelmed by the sense that she didn't have a home, frustrated over the puzzle of Maddie's seizures, and angry at God for letting her little one suffer.

Compound those emotions with the fact that this marked the first time she had returned to the Desolation Wilderness area since her search for her father's plane. Her defenses were weakened. She'd have been lying if she said she didn't long for a companion. Someone to lighten the load and to hold her and to know her.

Matthew 6:33. She knew it by heart. The promise had encouraged her ever since she'd become a single mother. The Lord knew what she needed. Seek first His kingdom, and the things she needed would be added to her as well. If Silas still wanted a chance with her, he'd have to show that he had the right priorities.

She never released her feelings for him. They just got bottled and stored away and, she had thought, left to ferment in the recesses of her heart. She knew when she married Seth that at some point—decades later, if she'd had her way—she'd have to open that bottle of memories. She planned to wait until time brought it beyond any intoxicating sweetness and then pour out the pungent vinegar it had become. No longer a risk. No longer too much of a heartache.

But Seth had been a lie. And here she was, drawing from cellared emotions. Sitting with Silas and twisting the corkscrew into the walls she'd put up. The ensuing bouquet, at first pungent, now decanted and relaxed.

She realized she had been silent for a while. Silas smiled, eliciting a grin from her. She looked down and cut a bite of pork. *Breathe. Get a grip.*

A familiar man's voice, tense and short, came from behind her. "Captain Westmore."

She turned to see Chief Weathers. Concern etched his brow.

"Chief. Hi. Is everything okay?"

He shook his head.

Madison. "What's happened? Has she had another seizure?"

He lifted a palm. "She's stable right—"

"Stable? Is she at the hospital?"

"Barton Memorial. In the ER."

Elle placed her napkin on the table. "Silas, I'm sorry. I need to go."

He rose. "I'll come with you."

"No. I mean . . . thank you, but I think I need to go on my own." Disappointment and disquiet filled his face. But she wasn't ready for him to share any more of her life. It was all she could do right now to not fall apart.

Her eyes turned hot. She turned to Weathers. "Can you drive me?"

"Absolutely." He nodded to Silas. "Mr. Kent."

CHAPTER 19

Bo had never touched a needle and spool before becoming a smokejumper. Funny how something like your life being on the line, literally, made one acquire and master a skill.

He'd found a seat at a table in the far corner of a classroom area set aside for jumpers. Old steel lockers lined one wall, an ancient blackboard on another with a reeled map above it dangling a cord. Over that hung a circular, black-rimmed clock that clicked with every movement of the minute hand. Monte sat with his feet up on a table watching a corner-mounted television broadcast the evening news—flashes of hundred-foot evergreens engulfed in flame and wide-angle shots of staggered lightning bolts striking ground. Sippi and Rapunzel played cribbage at another table. Their conversation was quiet but not particularly guarded and was well within Bo's earshot.

Rapunzel inserted a peg into the cribbage board. "He's got a plan, Sip. That's what you've got to understand."

Sippi shook his head. "I still don't get how it's all supposed to come together."

Bo threaded his needle along a seam in his secondary backup chute. He kept his ear inclined. Caleb had kept a distance from him since returning from the field. And Bo remained quiet. No waves. No protests. With Cleese sharpening his knife at every opportunity, Monte looming in the shadows, and these two cackling hyenas prowling about, it didn't give him much choice. None of those guys had the safety of their families to worry about.

Rapunzel drew a card. "We've got a small window of opportunity to jump. Then conditions won't allow anything near us for a bit."

Sippi spit tobacco in an empty soda can. "Sounds like it could be good cover."

"Long as we don't get surrounded and burned over."

Bo stretched. "I'm about to get some dinner. You boys heading over?" He hoped not. He wasn't even particularly hungry. Not since the other night.

Neither of them looked up, simply grunting "no" replies.

Bo put away his sewing kit, took a moment to admire the stitching on his reinforced seam, and then stowed the backup chute, only half listening as he prepared to leave.

Sippi laughed.

Rapunzel, irritated, said, "What're you guffawing about?"

"You sit there and you think you know everything, but you ain't even got the slightest clue what I been doing all afternoon before this, do you?"

Bo turned slowly toward the conversation. A look of consternation tightened Rapunzel's face. "You were sharpening your shovel in the hangar. With Cleese."

Bo unfolded and refolded his chute, buying time.

Sippi shook his head, still laughing. "You just figure me for an ignorant backwoods hick, don't you?"

"Two out of three ain't bad."

Sippi leaned forward, forearms on the table. "You know I was a journeyman apprentice electrician before I started fighting fire? I understand amps and voltage. I know how to wire things."

Rapunzel's chair creaked. "What kind of things?"

Sippi grinned. "Devices."

Rapunzel straightened.

"The kind that go—" Sippi arced his hands away from each other with spread fingers.

Bo finished folding his chute and stored it in a bag at the corner. The attention of the two meandered toward him, their eyes following him as he walked out of the room.

He nodded. "See you jokers when I see you."

Bo strode down the shadowed hall, the unsettling feeling of daggers being flung at his back. He avoided the cafeteria, his stomach still twisting from the previous night's horrors.

CHAPTER 20

Caleb would take an MRE any day over the jerky and slop in front of him. Who was in charge of logistics, anyway? Dry pork chops and pea soup. He sipped ice water from a paper cup. At least that was decent. Clear, pure Lake Tahoe snowmelt.

He eyed their new spotter across the room. Sitting alone after being ditched by the pilot.

Shivner sat several tables down, stuffing his face, hobnobbing with Command staff. Looking for ways to build himself up in their eyes. He was supposed to get them out of having a replacement. The desk jockey obviously wasn't up to the task. Caleb was holding up *his* end of things—had already secured transport out for them and their cargo. The shirt buttons across the guy's belly looked like they were about to shoot off. From over a shoulder his eyes met Caleb's. He chewed, wiped his face with a napkin, and broke the gaze. Caleb shook his head and dunked a slice of pork in the soup. He held it there, impatiently, hoping to instill some kind of moisture back into the irradiated meat.

This plan was supposed to be his break. He'd been waiting for it for a lifetime. Everything had led up to it. And now, on the cusp of attaining it, he had to deal with the incompetence of a pear-bodied coward. Shivner's two redeeming values? The spot-on latitude and longitude coordinates he'd related to Caleb—and his wisdom in choosing Caleb to be his point man.

How the fat slob ever survived a team-building Forest Service backpacking expedition through the Desolation Wilderness still escaped Caleb. It was highly probable that Shivner was struggling to keep up and was too embarrassed to be left behind, but being arrogant, stubborn, and a poor team player, he had broken off from the group of high-ranking individuals to "show them." A foolish move, but were it not for his excursion off of the established trail route, Shivner would have never wandered eighteen miles into veritably untrod wilderness and stumbled, literally, into the find.

Shivner had fractured his ankle in the process, and hiking out on it caused irreparable harm to the joint. Knowing he wouldn't be able to make a return trip to the cache deep in rough National Forest Service land, Shivner couldn't figure out how to furtively gain the treasure. But when the recent dry lightning cells stormed through and the Desolation Complex blew up, he saw his chance.

He'd called Caleb into his makeshift office, locked the door, and reclined in a squeaking seventies-vintage chair behind an avocado-and-mustard-colored metal desk. He played his game like a man who only had one good card to play, drawing out the story of his prized knowledge of an invaluable secret. He claimed he wasn't inclined to divulge it to just anybody—only to a man like Caleb, who was cunning and shrewd and capable enough on two good ankles to deliver the goods.

Caleb remembered almost getting up and walking out at that point. Shivner's posturing bordered on ridiculous. And Caleb was sure that whatever the man had discovered was probably ancient news on the Internet or the substance of native folklore.

The pompous bag of wind must've seen impatience in Caleb's face, because the moment before Caleb was about to rise, Shivner blurted out the secret.

"Gold." His irises quivered, lips testing the air to form the next word. "Chest after chest of raw gold. A hidden nineteenth-century cache of it."

Barely holding back incredulous laughter, Caleb stood to leave.

"No joke." Shivner fished keys from his pocket and reached down to a locked drawer in his desk.

He lifted from it two rocks and set them down with a heavy thud on the desktop. Both appeared to be pinecone-sized chunks of unrefined gold.

Perspiration beaded at the bridge of the man's nose. His breathing became heavy. "It's the Independence Find, Caleb. Has to be. *This* was all I could pack out. I'm lucky to have made it."

"You're talking legends." Caleb leaned over the desk and lifted the rock, hastening to bring his other hand under to support the weight. The heaviness for its size was shocking, at least forty pounds in his palms. "The Independence mine isn't anywhere near where you were hiking."

"I know. It's forty-five miles west of there."

"In ruins. I've been there."

"Fourth-grade field trip?"

"Fifth, actually."

"And so, like everybody, you heard the legend of the slave-labor conditions imposed on immigrants by the proprietor brothers and the string of accidents and deaths that befell them."

"The supposed cursed gold."

"Right. After the death of one brother and the other brother's wife, the mine was shut down and—"

"A large amount of the mined gold disappeared. It's an old story. What's your point?"

"I found a bunker, Caleb. An underground cache lined wall to wall with wooden chests of gold ore—just like these."

Caleb sat back in his chair and studied the man. "Say I believed you. How long have you known about this?"

"Two years."

"Two? Why haven't you—"

"Think about it. It's Forest Service land. The sheer weight of the cache. The logistics of getting to it and getting it out . . . No one could know I brought it out."

Caleb sat straight. He glanced back at the closed door and visually swept the room.

"Don't worry. No bugs. No cameras."

Caleb swallowed. "What're you proposing?"

"We may never have another chance like this. Mother Nature's gone and done us a huge favor. Put on a light show and coughed up a conflagration. The Forest Service has everything with wheels and rotors and wings out on missions to corral this complex, and so far, it's only been getting bigger, pushing them away. The Command staff is scrambling on their ends and elbows. It all makes out for a perfect—"

"Smoke screen."

Shivner pulled a bandana from his shirt pocket and wiped the sweat from his nose and cheeks. "Since it has been two years, before I commit anything in the way of resources to extricate it, we'll need to make sure the cache is still there. I'll need a tally of how much."

"Why me?"

"For one, it's your crew. Pendleton has had a penchant for hiring—what shall I call them?—rehabilitated disreputables."

"You calling me disreputable?"

"You did leave your last two jobs under less-than-ideal circumstances."

Pendleton had been instrumental in getting Caleb's foot in the door with the Forest Service. "Go on."

"These men, like you, are likely to recognize and seize an opportunity when presented with it. Pendleton, for all his good intentions, is also naïve. If executed correctly, this whole plan can happen without him being aware."

"You still haven't answered my question. Why me? Specifically?"

" 'Cause I know you. I'm a listener, and you've never hidden the fact that you hate your father. How many times have you griped about how he loves finances more than you? You want to prove you are the better man. This is your break."

Caleb considered punching the arrogant slob, but the guy was starting to sound interesting. "I'm listening."

"Don't you get it, son? This is your chance. 'Til now, you've followed the path of your heart without worry about money. Anybody knows you don't get into this business for the dough. But here opportunity stands before you—the chance to not only have your cake and eat it, but to shove a fat piece right in your father's face in the process."

Caleb huffed. "Shiv, I always figured you to be fat, dumb, and happy. I stand corrected on one account. You are a positively *miserable* person." Caleb rose and clunked the gold rock on the desk. "This is the most reckless idea I have ever heard." He let a grin escape at the corner of his mouth. "Sign me up."

Blinking his way out of the memory, Caleb pushed away from the table and dumped the rest of his meal in the trash.

Enough reminiscing—he had work to do.

CHAPTER 21

Elle let herself cry all the way to the hospital. Better to get it out before arriving at the ER. She didn't want Maddie to see her falling apart.

She flipped down the passenger seat visor in Weathers's SUV. No mirror. They came to a stop sign and she placed a hand on the rearview. "May I?"

"Of course."

She turned the mirror toward her and wiped the mascara runs from her cheeks. Red spider webs streaked the corners of her eyes.

Weathers parked the SUV but left the engine running. "I'm sorry I can't stay."

She put a hand on his shoulder. "No, it's okay. Thank you for driving me."

She opened the car door and strode across the parking lot, the South Tahoe dusk inordinately warm. The sliding double doors at the ambulance entrance opened as a paramedic exited. She slid through and wandered into the emergency room. A doctor and nurse congregated around one room, where Carol Weathers stood with two young children beside her.

Elle hurried over. Carol surprised her with a caring embrace. Elle pulled away with an acknowledging smile and turned into the room.

The doctor stood over Maddie, dictating orders to a nurse who was jotting rapid notes onto a chart. "And have her Dilantin levels checked. Maintain a 100cc's an hour, TKO drip. If she lapses back into seizure we'll switch from Valium to Xanax—"

"Her Dilantin levels are fine." Elle squeezed past the doctor to Maddie's side. "And go with Versed if you have to control any future seizure activity. The Xanax knocks her out for too long."

The doctor, a tall, square-jawed man with wavy dark hair graying at the edges, raised his eyebrows. He glanced at the nurse. "Make that Versed, point two milligrams per kilogram to a max of seven. And keep with the Dilantin-level check."

The nurse noted it, clicked her pen, and held the chart to her bosom while she walked out of the room.

Elle felt the doctor's eyes on her.

"You're the mother, I presume?"

"Yes."

He wheeled up the physician's chair and sat on its edge. "A pediatric patient's best care is quite often a mother's intuition."

Elle turned a polite smile and looked at Maddie's cherubic face. Her hair stuck in moist strands to her forehead, eyes closed. She snored quietly. Elle held Maddie's wrist, her pulse tapping at a rapid rate. "It's me, baby. Mommy's here." She stroked her hair.

"How long is her postictal period, typically?"

"Her recoveries have been taking longer lately. Up to forty-five minutes before she's fully alert. I've been keeping a log. She's had three times as many seizures in the past two months as she did all last year."

"Is there ever any warning?"

"Like an aura?"

"Yes."

Elle kept her hand over Maddie's and turned. "She's told me that she'll feel a storm coming, in her head. If she senses rain in the storm she knows it will be okay, that the feeling will wash over her and leave."

"And if she doesn't sense 'rain'?"

"Then it falls like lightning."

The doctor clicked his pen and scrawled on his clipboard. "Has she had these since birth?"

"Since she was three."

"And she's five now."

Elle nodded. "I've always been there when she wakes. As confused as she'll be, she always recognizes me. I'm like her anchor."

He studied Maddie. "Any bouts of status epilepticus?"

"Status what?"

"It's where a patient will suffer multiple attacks without a returning level of lucidity between them. It can be life-threatening."

"No. She's only ever had one at a time."

"With these lengthening postictal periods, there is an increased risk for her to fall into it. Who's your neurologist?"

"Mommy?"

Elle drew a breath and turned. Madison's pupils focused.

"Hi, Mommy."

Elle lifted her daughter to her chest and held her tight. "Hey, baby. Here I am. Mommy's here for you."

CHAPTER 22

Bo wandered down a narrow hall and out into the waning hues of daylight, along the tarmac, past dormant aircraft.

He thought he'd learned to read people better. It saved him plenty of times growing up. Now it wasn't just himself he was worried about. That made the situation unbearable.

He sat on a bench outside of the airport wall. A bird's nest perched at a corner alcove of the building, small chicks stretching their sinewy necks up on occasion, squeaking for their mother.

Images of violence from the night before shot through his mind. He looked away and swallowed.

Lightning burst. A new sheet of evening draped over the sky, mauve with fading blues. Distant thunder rumbled. A cloud-to-cloud burst of white shot out and vanished. Bo started walking again, and soon he stood outside the metal door to Jumper 41's hangar. His stomach tightened like a wrung-out towel.

He didn't like the sound of Sippi and Rapunzel's conversation. It wouldn't hurt to inspect and double check the equipment and the aircraft and—

Muted voices carried through the door.

Bo held his breath and inclined his ear. He stared at the steel door handle, waiting for it to move. The voices rose, then hushed, then continued again. He pressed his earlobe against the dusty metal door.

He heard the buzzing sound of the ceiling-hung halogen

lights. A fan blew. And then the voices again, the words recognizable, the inflections distinct—Caleb and Cleese.

"And I'm telling you that he ain't the kind of spotter to stay on the plane—no matter what." Caleb's voice.

"How can you know?"

"Because, he jumps with Adams. *The* Warren Adams. Besides, they've got an incident spotter now."

"A what?"

"I know. What timing, huh?"

"So he gets taken out too."

"You act like it's nothing." There was a pause. Bo looked over the empty tarmac. Caleb's voice picked up. "Folks are buying the burnover. We're not being investigated. Conditions are extreme, and everyone knows accidental death goes with the territory. But we show up again without our spotter, saying some 'accidental' tree knocked him off a cliff or some bull like that, you think anybody's going to believe us? We'll go to prison, Cleese. For a long, long time."

"I can handle the joint."

"You're not getting it."

"You're saying we buy him off?"

"I don't think he'll be game."

"Everybody can be bought."

"Can't take that chance. An accident is still the only way. But it has to look like an impartial accident, one that could've killed us all."

"I'm already ahead of you on that, Cay. I had Sippi wire up a couple special surprises."

"Can Sippi work with the kind of precision we need?"

"Guess we'll find out."

Caleb cursed. Bo heard footsteps, like pacing.

Cleese said, "We'll need it to coincide with the drop point we're aiming for. When our new spotter's in the cockpit, navigating, I'll slice his chutes.

"If everything goes well, we should have the following forty-eight hours of impassable fire weather to serve as smoke screen. They shouldn't even be able to get a rescue helicopter close until after we've liberated the gold."

The footsteps grew louder. Bo tiptoed back along the shadowed building wall and ducked behind a fifty-five-gallon drum. The door opened and the two stepped out.

"What about the others?" Cleese said.

"I've got them. Bo's the only one we need to keep an eye on. But some things motivate stronger than money."

CHAPTER 23

Elle opened her eyes. Her forehead rested square on the glass front of the vending machine she'd been staring into when she dozed off, on her feet. She leaned back, rubbed her brow, and glanced to either side. Nobody around. Except for that black security camera pointed right at her. She simpered, sure she'd given a security guy a good laugh.

What was she getting? Right. A Skor bar. The last one too. A-5. The metal corkscrew spun, and the candy bar tilted, then stopped. Halted from its fall by the spiral endpiece. She tapped the glass, then pushed on the metallic front. Before she knew it, she was rocking the entire vending machine back and forth. She stopped, stood back, and stared at the one thing she wanted in that stupid seven-foot box.

What are we doing here?

Elle filled a paper cup with water and shuffled back toward Maddie's room. Only twenty feet away, with the door chocked open. She wanted to be sure she could hear her if she woke. The doctor had admitted Maddie for observation, although her Dilantin levels came back fine, just like Elle told them they would, and even though Maddie became more coherent, though physically exhausted. The lone floor nurse filled out a chart behind the counters of the center work area farther down the wide hallway. Elle caught a glimpse of the clock. Two thirty-seven AM. What was she doing? Staying up was not going to help Maddie get better. Even though it was irrational, she felt that by being there she could somehow keep her child from lapsing into another seizure. Like when a sports fan is certain his team will lose if he doesn't cheer them on.

The doctor had said it was especially crucial in the first few hours that Maddie didn't fall back into a series of seizures. They were past that point now. And the Versed seemed to have worked. But since no one could tell her exactly what was truly causing the seizures, who was to say it would work next time?

They'd been through this so many times. Treating the symptoms. Discharging. Then another seizure and they ended right back in the hospital. Symptoms treated. Discharged. No closer to a cure than they'd been.

Elle stepped into the room, carefully tapping the doorstop aside with her toe. She set down the water cup, found the convertible sleeping chair beside Maddie's bed and sank into it. Parking-lot light shot through the edge of the window blinds across Elle's face. She adjusted to an uncomfortable position to avoid it. Maddie lay in peaceful repose. Softly snoring with Rose, brought earlier by Carol Weathers.

Elle wanted to take Maddie someplace safe. A place where five-year-old girls didn't suffer unexplained seizures. Where picturesque mountainsides didn't swallow up loved ones. Someplace where the world wasn't on fire.

An early encounter with Silas drifted into her thoughts.

She'd been riding her bicycle on base, back from an errand and simple picnic on her own. Guys at McCall thought of her mostly as a thick-skinned pilot who knew puddle-jumping aircraft like nobody else. That was her father coming out in her. And she was those things. But she also relished the opportunity to simply be a girl. And that had almost always required getting away from the base. Even if it was for something as simple as a bike ride to the bookstore and a reading picnic on the sandy banks of Payette Lake.

There was nothing manly about her bike, and she loved that about it. Basket on the front, big curvy handlebars, and only one gear. It was made for cruising.

Funny, really, how she'd made the trip on that bicycle in a skirt so many times before without catching it in the bike chain. It figured then that, just as she attempted to dismount her bike at the top of the wooden steps leading to her favorite pine-tree-shaded strip of beach, the hem of her white skirt would wind inextricably into the bike chain and gear teeth.

She found herself balancing on one toe, grasping the wooden railing to keep from tumbling down the steps, stuck in that position in quite the predicament when a voice startled her.

"Can I lend you a hand?"

It was the guy from the Wing Stop the night before—the one with the cheesy line that almost won her over. Her gut instinct was to refuse. To wave him off. *Nah, thanks. I got it.* But she knew it would be ridiculous to do so, and being thankful for this stranger, this handsome friendly stranger and his timely intervention, she angled her eyebrows and with a pitiful smile responded, "Please."

He knelt by the gear linkage and inspected the entanglement, sandy blond hair dangling. He wore a navy blue T-shirt with the standard Forest Service–issue dark green pants.

"Thank you," she said. "I can't believe this happened."

He looked up. "Don't remember my name, do you?"

Elle racked her memory, but all she could think of was *Surfer Boy.*

"I used my best line on you, and you can't even remember my name the next day." He grinned and pulled a Leatherman multi-tool from a pouch on his belt. "I'm sure you don't need me to tell you that riding a bike in a long skirt is inherently dangerous."

"No. I'm well abreast of that fact now."

He loosened the nuts on the linkage, and she felt the tension on her skirt alleviate a bit as he adjusted the wheel and lifted the chain off the gear teeth. A shark-tooth grease pattern unveiled on her dress as he unwrapped it.

He handed her the hem. "Look at that. Not even torn."

Elle cocked her head in semi-amazement. "I was getting ready to take a knife to the darn thing."

He eyed her. "You carry a knife?"

"Maybe."

He stood, wiped his hand off, and offered it. "Silas Kent."

She shook and cleared her throat. "Elle Westmore." She gave a coy smile. "But you knew that."

"Couldn't forget it." He knelt again by the bike and put the wheel-and-gear-chain assembly back together.

As much as Elle hated to admit it—having grown up near the McCall base and not being willing to date firefighters—her options had been limited. And here was just another smoke-jumper. A charming one, no doubt. But was anything really different with him? She had debated the best way to find out more about him without it seeming that she was too interested. And as he set the wheel in place, she knew she was about to lose her chance.

"So, are you here for a while?" Elle rolled her eyes at herself the instant it came out.

"Funny you'd ask," Surfer Boy said. "Our base is getting a massive remodel, and instead of relegating us south to the Shack, we'll be located here the rest of the summer." He set the chain and stood. "There you go—like new."

Southern Idaho. The smokejumper shack. . . . "You were the one who showed me around the new Twin Otter."

"And you were the one in the summer dress."

She felt her cheeks burn hot. "Well, thank you, again." Brushing off her hands, she grabbed the handlebars and seat to guide her bike down the wooden steps.

"Hey." He cleared his throat.

She paused. "Mm-hmm?"

"Maybe we can do this again . . . sometime." An awkward smile creased his lips.

She bit her bottom lip and smiled.

Elle's cell phone rattled on the nightstand.

She snatched it up and silenced it. Maddie turned in bed and mumbled.

Elle held the cell to her ear and stood. "Hello?"

"Elle, this is Weathers."

She eased the door handle loose, edged it open, and squinted with the brighter hallway lighting. "One second." She slid through. "Can you hear me okay?"

"You're a little scratchy. How am I coming across?"

"Fine. Fine. What time is it?" She searched for the wall clock and found one far off, though the numbers were too fuzzy to read.

"Ten to four."

Elle arched her stiff back. Strange that Weathers would call her so early. "What—" She cleared her throat. "What's up?"

"We need you here."

"Where? At the base?"

"You're scheduled to fly a crew out in two hours."

"What? They were talking about nine o'clock."

"The fire blew up again. Big time. They estimate it spread another thousand acres since nightfall."

Elle rubbed an eyebrow and pinched wiry hair strands back. She didn't know what to say. "Chief, I . . . I can't. I'm still here with Madison."

"I know. I've got Carol on her way right now."

She shook her head. "I can't leave her."

"Elle, you are the only one who can fly this mission."

"There are a dozen pilots on this fire. You can't tell me every single one of them is unavailable."

"It's not that they're unavailable. It's the conditions and the terrain. This thing is creating its own weather, Elle. I'm shutting down all air attack today. Grounding everything we've got. Nothing flies after the start of the new operational period at oh-seven-hundred hours."

Elle pinched the bridge of her nose.

The line rustled. "If we don't get another jumper crew on that eastern flank, it'll make an unrestrained run straight for the residential communities in South Lake. We'll lose hundreds of homes."

She tilted her head against the wall.

"Elle, I need you for this. No one knows these mountains like you. I watched you pore over those topos every night for three weeks. I'm willing to bet you've logged more immediate flight time over that particular patch of planet Earth than anyone alive.

"Let's turn your father's passing into something positive. Something that can help save lives and homes. What do you say?"

Elle covered her mouth and nose. A tear trickled down to her finger. She peeked in Maddie's room. Her daughter lay in the same position she'd been in. The double doors opened at the end of the hall, and Carol walked through with two sleepy-eyed children still in their pajamas.

"Okay." Elle took a deep breath. "For Dad."

CHAPTER 24

Silas studied the grim faces seated in the crew compartment. Their expressions beyond game faces. Scowls. Gnarls. The bulkhead vibrated against his arm. The whole plane reeked of B.O. and acrid smoke. He leaned back from the bulkhead and sat beside Elle in the cockpit. Her eyes danced between flight gauges and the cauliflower expanse before them, anvil-shaped thunder cells building on the horizon.

Silas seated his headset and positioned the microphone. "You sure we got a crew of jumpers and not a con-crew?"

Her lips drew upward. "You've never flown with any of these guys?"

"Have you?"

She peered over her aviator glasses.

"Right. I guess there's not a jumper in the continental U.S. you haven't flown with at some point, huh?" He rubbed the back of his neck. "Maybe this spotter thing's just got me out of my element."

"Just think, 'What Would Warren Do?' "

"I'll make a wristband."

"You learned from the best."

The cockpit rattled. Flashes of lightning lit the horizon. Elle took off her aviators and hooked them on the shell necklace dangling from the feet of the hula dancer on the dash. Wrinkles of concern tightened at the corners of her eyes.

"What is it?"

"Hmm?"

"What's on your mind?"

She opened her mouth to speak and then paused and looked out her side windows. Greens and browns dotted granite ridgelines.

"This is the first time I've flown over this territory. . . ."

"The first?"

She shot an impatient look. "Since . . ."

Silas nodded in realization. "Since your father."

"Yeah."

"I'm so sorry."

Elle bit her bottom lip and worked up a smile. "You don't have to be."

A lightning salvo struck a mountain peak in the near distance.

Silas squinted, discerning a thin black column rising into the air. "I think that last one might have taken out the radio tower."

Elle glanced between the smoke and her radio equipment. She depressed the transmit button. "South Lake Tower, this is Jumper 41. How do you copy?"

Silas listened. "Press the button again."

She complied. Silas watched her press it but heard nothing. "You're not hitting the radio repeater."

"No." Elle flipped toggle switches and angled the plane toward their ten o'clock. "Probably best we fly around that active cell. When we approach the drop zone, we can see if we're able to hit the next closest repeater."

The plane leveled. Silas fidgeted in his seat. What was he doing in the cockpit anyway? This was Warren's job.

Elle pointed to a stretch of land beyond the windshields. "I must've flown over that patch of earth fifty times."

"Is that where you think he went down?"

"Best guess. Based on his flight plan, last radio contact, fuel, and . . . I don't know, just hunches."

"The way you sensed he would fly?"

She seemed to consider his words and nodded. "Yeah."

Silas readjusted his headset. "I remember him well. Like the time you brought me over to your house for dinner."

"And he showed you his gun collection."

"Classic. He oiled his shotgun barrel, all casual like, right there in the living room while we chatted."

She laughed.

"He was a good man, Elle. I flew with him once. That next summer, I mean."

"After we . . ."

"Yeah."

Thunder boomed, rolling across the clouds like a freight train.

"Where?"

"On the east Alaskan complex."

"Did he—"

"Recognize me? Oh yeah."

"No. That's not what I was going to ask."

"Sorry. Did he . . ."

"Tell you to meet him out behind the hangar?"

Silas laughed. Scattered rain pelted the windshields.

Elle's expression remained unchanged.

He drew in his smile. "No. No. He was very amiable. But he held my gaze long when he shook my hand. His hands were rough and strong like a vise grip. I had the feeling he was only shaking with a fraction of his strength. That he could've broken the bones in my hand if he'd decided to."

A comforted expression warmed her face.

Silas scratched the corner of his jaw. "Glad to see that pleases you. The thought of my metacarpals being shattered."

She threw him a sideways glance.

"He asked how I'd been. I told him I'd tied in with Warren Adams in Alaska and was committed to going where he went."

"What did he say to that?"

"He said commitment is a powerful thing."

The cockpit shuddered. Elle glanced at the gauges.

"He told me you were married." Silas studied the mushrooming smoke column on the horizon. Half a dozen smaller gray pillars billowed from the earth around them. "And I asked him to tell you something. I don't know if he ever did." He drew a deep breath. "You know that I didn't have a family growing up, that the San Mateo Home for Boys was the only home I knew."

She nodded.

"I never told you about a lady who would visit there. Every other Friday. Everyone called her Grandma Jo. She read to us. She remembered all our birthdays and would give us gifts. Little things, now that I look back on it. But we barely had any toys of our own. So her gifts were treasures to me. She had eyes that smiled. You know what I mean? Rich, earthy. With rosy freckled cheeks beneath them. Long after she finished reading, I'd find reasons to stay by her and talk. She'd listen to my stories about baseball and whittling wood, and she would ooh and ah over my rock collection."

"She sounds like a true grandmother."

"She was, for me. Sort of like a mother too. The closest thing I'd known to one."

Elle glanced at a peak at their ten o'clock. She angled the wings slightly westward.

"It wasn't right for me to leave you that summer, Elle. I know that. I can't change what I did, or what all came of it. But I was scared. I felt like our relationship was on a precipice, and . . . too many times in the past I thought a family would work out for me only to find out that I wasn't really worth the people's time." He ran his hand across his mouth. "I had no idea what it was like to be part of an actual family. And at the end of that summer, right when I was teetering on all those fears, I got word from a caretaker at the San Mateo Home—Grandma Jo had suffered a stroke and was in the ICU.

"I know it wasn't right to leave you. It's no excuse. It was the worst possible timing, the worst decision I've ever made." He swallowed. "I freaked out. I made it my reason to leave. The season was winding down and the base manager gave me leave to visit her." He drew his fingers over his brow. "I shouldn't have left like that." *Shouldn't have even left.* "I tried so many times to call but ended up dangling pay-phone receivers every time."

They flew in silence for a while. The buzzing hum of the engines behind them. The wind whistled through thin crevices in the window seals.

Elle depressed the radio's transmit button. "Air ops, this is Jumper 41 with a location update." She waited, turned the radio-frequency dial a notch and tried again.

No response.

"Hmm . . ." She flipped a switch and leveled the plane at a new altitude. "He did, you know."

171

Silas cast a curious glance.

She caught his eye. "He did tell me."

A bright light burst.

The plane banked hard. It groaned and roared. Smoke ribbons flailed over the windshield. Elle gripped the rattling yoke one handed, grasping the throttle with her other.

Silas clutched his seat. "What's happening?"

"We lost an engine."

Altitude sank. Silas's stomach jumped. The other wing engine roared at high RPMs. The horizon thunderheads appeared higher than before.

Bo barreled through the bulkhead. "We got an engine on fire."

The ALT gauge spun counterclockwise. Silas threw a look to Elle. "How close are we to the drop zone?"

"What?"

He shouted. "How close to the drop zone?"

"Eleven, maybe twelve miles."

Silas stood, grasping the seat back, and said to Bo, "Toss me that topo map."

Bo fetched the rolled cylinder and handed it to him without letting go. He stood face-to-face, staring at him, and unzipped the front of his jumpsuit. From it he produced a compact square canvas pouch bound by thick straps. "Don't lose this."

An emergency chute? Why did Bo think he needed a backup to his existing chutes? He'd strap them on when it was time to make the jump. He'd gone through everything that morning, like he always did. But the man wouldn't let go of the topo map until Silas acknowledged him, unzipped his own jumpsuit, and placed the chute inside.

Bo released the cylinder and stood back. "We can reel it out on the floor here."

A panel screw rattled loose and tumbled across the floor. Silas pried open the cylinder and fished out the map. Bo smoothed it out on the floor. The lines levitated with the vibrating floor. Silas blinked them into focus and let his fingers find the airport and then traced the route he'd penciled in the night before. He had scribed estimated time signatures every five miles. Just like Warren always did.

"That puts us around . . ." Silas tapped the paper. "Here."

"By Crystal Lake?" Elle yelled over the din.

"Yes. But Crystal Pond is more like it. Pretty tiny. Any meadows around?"

"Still a ways off. Mostly hillsides and tree stands. Here." She stretched a hand back. "Show it to me."

Silas folded the map to isolate their location and held it in front of her. Sweat beaded at the bridge of his nose. "Can't you limp her back to South Lake?"

"No. One engine can't hang at this altitude."

"What're you going to do?"

"Set her down in that puddle."

"Can you reach—"

The plane dropped altitude again. Silas sucked in a breath.

Elle adjusted the throttle to a buzz-skip sound from the remaining engine. "I'll have to. Have your boys make the jump now."

"Too forested. We'll wait 'till you're over—"

"No way. I'm heading in at too steep an angle as it is." Then, under her breath, "Be lucky if I even clear the ridge."

Silas hesitated.

"I got this, Kent. Here, show me the map again."

He held it up.

"There." She pointed to a patch of light green. "We'll be over that in about forty-five seconds."

"Too small."

"It's all you got."

Caleb shouted from the bulkhead, "Let's get off this bird."

Silas stumbled back into the crew compartment. He grabbed Caleb by the chest harness. "Line up for the door. No time for paracargo, so everyone take a hand tool. Let's move."

Jumpers scrambled. Last second gear adjustments and the linking of yellow tether lines for chute deployment. They gathered by the jump door, and Silas cranked it open. An immediate blast of heated orange and choking black smoke poured in. Silas ducked low, holding his breath and hiding his face in the crook of his elbow. He crouched beneath the smoke and peered downward for the drop point. He spotted a dime-sized patch of green between the trees.

Three separate smoke columns bordered the area. Even with a successful jump, they could be hemmed in by the fire.

Sunlight glinted off a creek bed. His eyes traced it through the forest, winding like a snake down a nearby ridge from Crystal Lake. Could work as a safety zone when things got hot.

It was as good as they were going to get.

Silas waved Caleb forward and pointed out the landing zone. Caleb glanced at Silas's chute pack still hanging from the fore bulkhead.

Silas waved. "I'll be fine. You see the spot?"

Caleb nodded and placed his hands on the doorframe. Silas counted off with a hand in the air. One. Two. Three.

He patted Caleb's leg. He shot like a cannonball through the smoke. Silas strained to track him through the sky. A broad white chute popped into view.

Cleese stood next in the doorway. The plane shifted, and Silas caught balance against the wall. He pointed, got the nod, and gave the three-count. Leg pat. Second jumper out.

Silas repeated the sequence until all five were off. He stood and exhaled.

He didn't plan on joining them.

The plane angled steeper. Silas caught himself at the jump door, partway out in the slipstream. He clawed his way back in and clambered to the cockpit. "How long do we have?"

"What're you still doing here?"

"The jumpers are off."

"But you're here."

"I'm not going to leave you."

"Your duty is with them."

"My place is with you."

Her hands flurried between the yoke, the throttle lever, and panel switches.

Silas braced a hand on the ceiling and the other on the seatback. The groaning descent loudened. He caught a view of a large mountain ridge approaching fast.

"I'm not going to leave you again."

She stared into his eyes. The plane dipped. "Go shut the jump door."

"Got it."

The cabin seesawed. Silas staggered through the bulkhead and slammed against the wall by the door. He reached out for the latch handle, nearly reaching it when the plane tipped to the opposite side.

He tumbled, smacking into the porthole windows. The remaining engine blared. Tarry smoke and flames rolled past the open door. The plane dove and tipped back to the jump-door side.

The earth spun into view. Silas's feet flipped out from under him. He fell across the cabin and snagged the edge of the outer door handle. His legs dropped outside, raging wind pulling at his calves. He clawed, fingertips slipping from the handle. Smoke billows engulfed. The door slammed shut and the slipstream caught hold, sucking him into the sky.

CHAPTER 25

He tumbled like a gyroscope. The world spun in stark blues, browns, and greens. An arm flailed out, deploying like a wing that worsened the spinning. The pressure in his head intensified. A crimson veil coated his vision. Silas forced out his other arm to stabilize the spin. Time meant altitude, and he should have already had a chute deployed.

Wind roared in his ears. The red in his eyes darkened to an encroaching black. The gyrating lessened, and he fought to bring an arm back in. It slammed into his chest. He worked his fingers to the zipper on his jumpsuit and pulled it down just enough to grasp the emergency chute Bo had given him.

How had he known?

Air ballooned his jumpsuit. Silas worked his hand inside and grasped the chute straps. He brought his other arm in, tumbling more as he did so. He fought a pressure in his head that morphed into lightness.

Working his arms into the straps, the chute pouch across his chest, he threaded one of the remaining straps around his leg and fought to clip it in place on the chute pack.

The red in his vision began to whiten. An airy and ethereal feeling filled his mind. The sound of the rushing air lessened. The whizzing colors of the planet washed into the dusk of his peripheral vision. It all became very comfortable and somnolent and enticing.

All he had to do was close his eyes.

Click. The leg strap locked in place. He blinked to focus. The forest flew toward him, flanked by bulbous smoke columns. No time for the other strap.

He yanked the ripcord handle. A flapping green snake unfurled into the sky. It wagged and whipped like a dragon kite.

Open.

Come on . . . Open.

The ground blurred with scattered views of craggy mountaintops and boulders and jutting treetops.

Ope—

Wind billowed the chute, widening like an umbrella. It torqued the flimsy shoulder straps and dug deep into his leg tendons.

Streaking colors coalesced. The air quieted. Earth approached.

No creek bed in sight. No meadow. No lake.

With little to no ability to steer his chute, he'd have to thread between the fast-approaching pines below him, hoping for a clear shot to the forest floor.

Jumper 41 disappeared behind a distant mountain peak, its wing spewing pitch-colored smoke.

He turned his attention back below. With his speed of descent it was going to be a hard landing. With a decent buildup of pine-needle duff on the forest floor and a tight tuck and roll, he could do this, God-willing, without impaling himself on the way down.

The canopy drew near. Silas veered for a spot between a stand of five evergreens.

There was a showering of needles, the sound of breaking branches, and an abrupt, skull-jerking halt.

———————

Elle swallowed a scream at the sight of Silas's body tumbling through the air. He didn't have a chute.

Please, God, no.

The hull shook and rattled, blurring the flight gauges. Jumper 41 dropped again, increasing speed and elevating the groan of the remaining engine. Elle fought the stick to aim toward Crystal Lake, her faint hope to manage a water landing. She needed every cubic inch of lift, no measure for mistakes.

She feathered the controls and broadcasted through her headset, "Mayday, Mayday, Mayday. Jumper 41 going down with a critical engine failure. On trajectory toward Crystal Lake. Mayday, Mayday, Mayday."

Silence filled her headset. She threw it to the floor.

The choppy gray of Crystal Lake stretched into view just beyond the next ridgeline. The plane lost lift again, leaving her stomach a hundred feet higher.

The nose aimed at the ridge. If she tried to pull up farther she'd lose speed and more altitude. If she didn't change her current course, she'd never clear it. She would smash into the craggy granite before having the chance to put down in the water.

A scene with her father flashed in her mind—in the cockpit of his Cessna, puttering engine on one wing during their vacation in Canada. She had watched his hands, his face. Seconds before touching down he pushed forward on the stick.

Forward.

Gain speed. Draw altitude from the inertia and clear the last treetops.

Elle focused on the approaching landscape, her fist gripped

tight on the yoke. She judged the distance to the mountainside, jammed the throttle forward with one hand, and tipped the nose with the other. The plane dipped like a roller coaster, whining and moaning.

Wait.

The ground grew larger. Treetops like spearheads.

Wait.

Boulders and logs and pine-needle duff.

Now.

She jerked backward. The aircraft arced skyward. It climbed the air above the jutting hillside, momentum waning with increasing altitude until it crested and stalled straight above the peak.

Elle floated in her seat. Thick smoke ribbons waved over the windshield.

She feathered the stick forward and dropped toward the lake basin. A treetop struck a horizontal stabilizer on the tail section. The plane veered. Elle fought to keep the nose up, seesawing the wings. The lake rushed below. Maddie and Silas flashed through her mind, and she smashed into the surface with windshield-shattering force.

Silas opened his eyes, bringing into focus the verdant shadowing of the sun. A mosaic pattern of sunlight painted the forest floor far below. He breathed in scents of pine and woodsmoke and took in his immediate surroundings—the ribbed bark of the tree trunk ten feet from him, the thick evergreen branches his tangled chute dangled him from. Mountain blue jays squawked nearby. A chipmunk skittered headfirst down the tree Silas hung from. His neck ached with whiplash stiffness. He opened and closed his hands and tested his joints, which at his hips and shoulders felt as if they'd been stretched to their limits.

A limb snapped, jostling Silas lower. The branch fell fifty feet to the ground, frightening a bird from its roost. He didn't want to hang around to see how long this setup would hold.

Silas lifted his foot to reach the zipper pouch at his ankle. It bulged with the hundred feet of half-inch letdown rope that every jumper carried for just this predicament. His small movements produced a subtle sway and subsequent sounds of creaking wood above.

He took a deep breath. This was something he'd trained for. Something he'd been through before, though not so high. Getting stuck in a tree was usually a laughable thing for a jumper. One worthy of buying pie and ice cream for the crew after the mission. But this wasn't a situation of missing a perfectly good drop zone. And one could survive a two-story drop, but he dangled a good fifty feet off the ground.

The chute jerked a foot lower. Silas grabbed the straps. There was little chance the Swiss-cheese fabric his chute canvas had become would do much to slow his descent. If the limbs gave way, the best he could hope for was that he would get caught up in another set before smacking into the ground.

Bright side—if Bo hadn't given him the backup chute, Silas wouldn't even have the pleasure of dealing with his present problem.

He tied his letdown rope to the chute straps and then threaded it through an eight-plate attached to his suit for rappelling. By applying friction through twists in the rope, it would help him perform a controlled descent. He dropped the remainder of rope to the forest floor, watching it unravel like a snake. He slipped his arms from the chute harness and dangled, now suspended by the letdown line alone.

He loosened the tension on the rope and rappelled downward. At twenty feet he exhaled. At fifteen he grinned. At five feet he laughed.

Ground.

Silas knelt down, disconnected the rope from his jumpsuit, and grabbed two heaping fistfuls of pine-needle duff and kissed them.

———

Elle woke underwater, lungs screaming for oxygen. Giant air bubbles like jellyfish ejected out the windshield frames. She unlatched her seat harness, tore off her headset, and pushed off the captain's chair with her feet, following the air masses through the windshield and toward a waving band of sunlight.

She crested the surface and gasped for breath, waves splashing and smacking her in the face. Smoke and fire rolled off the surface of the water.

The floating fuel spill stretched around her, flames flashing across it. She paddled hard and fast, fueled by adrenaline, away from the fire and the sinking aircraft. She didn't let herself think about the burning in her lungs, the lightness in her head, and the fatigue in her arms. She strained against the weight of the pond pulling down on her clothing. She focused on one goal. One purpose. Escape the fire. Make the shore. Live.

Flames burst across her path, encircling her. She dropped beneath the surface, swimming down and forward, feeling the heat in the water as she submarined beneath the burning barrier.

Elle surfaced again, drawing air into her lungs. Beyond the

reach of the fuel, she shifted to her back, stroking along. Just like learning to swim with her dad. *Monkey, Tree, Rocket ship.*

Her foot struck a stone. Her other met the pond bottom. She turned to see the shore a dozen feet away.

She slogged forward, trudging through the shallows, and collapsed on a pebble-covered beach. Through the smoke, in the middle of the pond, the red aircraft tail with its white *41* sank out of view.

CHAPTER 26

Bo spat dirt and pine needles.

The sharp needles dug a mosaic into his palms. He lifted his hands, trembling, and turned with caution, evaluating his physiological status. Searing pain shot through his side. His hand met the hot ooze of blood soaking through his jumpsuit where a branch impaled him. He winced and ran his tongue across his salty lower lip. He touched the back of his hand to his mouth and inspected the spotted blood it came away with.

By God's grace he was alive. He could only pray that Silas Kent and the pilot found the same fortune. Bo had managed to find and disable one of the engine explosives before takeoff. It at least gave the pilot a fighting chance. If he'd just had time to get to the other . . .

Bo twisted to check his landing path. The view behind was nothing but trees, save for a ten-foot-wide lane—a smooth Slip 'N Slide of dirt. His torso was still tethered to the lengthened parachute cords, and the torn mess of a chute was caught on the lower branches of the trees at the beginning of the slide.

He replayed the moments before touchdown in his mind. He'd come in hot and fast, hoping to be able to slow up once he was positioned over an opening in the forest, but he was too low. Just as all seemed lost, a forceful wind directed him to the best clearing available.

His chute had caught the moment before he would have

struck a sequoia, and it seemed an invisible hand had directed him to the optimal landing spot.

The smell of smoke snapped his focus back. Fire wasn't far. A spider crept over the tree trunk in front of him. A light breeze cooled the sweat on his brow. He made out the subtle rippling of a nearby creek.

Disconnecting his harness, he worked out of his jumpsuit. Every movement exacerbated the pain in his flank, each vibration causing him to shudder with a stabbing sensation. He felt like pulling out the protruding branch, but his fundamental first-aid training told him not to, to stabilize a penetrating object in place.

He slid his Pulaski axe from his pack. Bo typically jumped with his tool rather than wait for the paracargo drop. Given the situation, it could become more of a weapon than a firefighting tool.

He sucked a pained breath through his teeth. The canopy was too thick and high to see beyond. Hard to know how far the fire was from him. The creek could provide shelter if it made a run. Keeping a hand on his side, he slumped to the ground and leaned back against a tree.

If only he could have undone the sabotage. He lacked both time and full knowledge. And a part of him hadn't been ready to believe they'd go through with their plan to blow the engines.

He believed now.

Caleb clearly wanted no survivors who weren't in on the plan. Cleese was a thorough saboteur, even cutting Silas's chutes in case he didn't go down with the plane.

Caleb had made his intentions clear, and his not-so-subtle hints drove deep. "Wouldn't want anything to happen to the twin sisters back home. Would you, Bo?"

Bo wasn't a man who needed things spelled out. It had taken everything in him not to grab Caleb by the throat.

"It's a dangerous job out there. I wonder how much it would take to make a guy like you never, ever, have to worry about his safety again."

A threat and a bribe. All behind a smiling veil.

Bo shook the memory from his head. He gritted his teeth and stood. The pain in his side wasn't going to get any better sitting there. With the emergency chute Bo had given Kent, there was still a chance he had survived.

If that was the case, Bo needed to rejoin the group before Kent did, for both their sakes.

CHAPTER 27

God wrote His law on every man's heart. Caleb had slogged through catechism. Whether resulting from indoctrination or genuine personal conviction, he didn't dispute the fact. He knelt in the small meadow by the creek bed, gathering his chute from the water, tracing with his eyes the smoke trail across the sky.

Caleb knew he was accountable for his actions. That truth wasn't relative. And while he could not presume to see the world as others did, he found it hard to believe that Cleese, who now stood in the stream working his arms out of his chute pack, possessed the same level of conviction. To him it seemed that Cleese's heart was so calloused and scarred that it lay immune to the twinge of guilt and the scraping pain of sin.

Maybe that made Caleb the worse of the two.

This was supposed to be about the money. About finders keepers and thumbing his nose at his father's suit-and-tie hedge-fund enterprises. But the blood of two men had been spilled. Add to that the likely deaths of a female pilot and their new spotter. How had he become responsible for four deaths in half as many days? Remarkable how the course of one's life could change in an instant.

He cleared his throat and spat. End result—what was done was done. He couldn't change that.

Caleb finished gathering his chute. He stored it with his

jumpsuit at the base of a tree along the edge of the clearing. A wave of thin smoke crept through the air overhead.

Cleese sloshed across the creek toward him. "I seen Sippi aiming to touch down 'bout a quarter mile ahead."

"All right. Let's grab what we need and tie in with him."

"What about the spotter?" Igneous eyes sat in the deep recess of his brow.

"If he did jump, it will have been soon after us."

Cleese grinned. "Must've been quite a surprise for him to find his chutes less than intact."

Caleb exhaled. "We'll tie in with the others and then split off in teams. Monte, Mansfield, and you will start a sweep for Kent's body. I, Sippi, and Rapunzel will collect the cache and start positioning it for the helicopter rendezvous. Meet up with us as soon as you can."

"You sure your pilot is good for it?"

"He can fly a Huey in heavy smoke like no one I've seen. He also happens to be drowning in debt. He has access to a bird and he needs the money."

"How much does he know?"

"Not a thing. Just that he's getting a fat chunk of change to pick up an undisclosed cargo and to keep his mouth shut about it. He won't talk."

Cleese cracked his neck. "Hopefully not. For his own good."

"You'd just love for him to give you a reason, wouldn't you?"

Cleese's cheeks lifted, revealing a grin accentuated by widely spaced teeth. "You know me well, good Parson."

———

Caleb found Sippi and Rapunzel about a quarter mile away, gathering up their chutes along the creek bed. They tied their jump gear to a nearby tree and fell in next to Cleese.

The smell of smoke grew stronger. Faint sounds of popping and crackling present in the near distance.

The sound of branches snapping came from behind a row of trees to the side of the creek. Bo Mansfield emerged, hand pressed against a branch protruding from his side.

Caleb walked up to him. "Canopy landing?"

"Not exactly."

Caleb looked close. "How bad is it?"

"You the medic."

"Let me see."

Bo pulled up his blood-soaked shirt. Caleb examined the entry wound. A half-inch diameter branch protruded about six inches from his flank. "How far in do you think it is?"

Bo gritted his teeth and felt around the side of his abdomen. "Three or four inches, maybe."

With only one engine explosion, they had been thrown off course—that left them miles to walk and less time to work with. Caleb needed Bo's manpower. He exhaled. "In the city I'd just stabilize it and the hospital would run an abdominal CT before attempting to pull it."

Bo stared, his face expressionless.

"Right," Caleb said. "But we're not in the city now, are we?" He looked again at the wound. "You may have lacerated your liver, perforated a bowel . . . There's really no way to know."

A hand stretched around Caleb and grabbed the branch.

Bo brought up his arm and shouted.

Cleese lifted a bloody stick in the air, smiling his gap-riddled grin. "Problem solved."

Bo pressed his fingers over the hole in his side. Blood oozed between them.

Caleb fished a bandana from his shirt pocket and pushed it firmly on the wound. "Keep pressure on that. I'm going to need you upright to accomplish our mission."

Bo grimaced and fixed his eyes on Cleese.

Cleese put his hands up and back-stepped. "Whoa, hey. Easy there, Bo. Just taking care of business. The good Parson here likes to deliberate a little long for my taste. Time's a wasting, and we still got another guy to find." He sidestepped, extending a hand toward the forest. "So if y'all don't mind, let's finish dressing our boo-boos and tie in with Monte so we can get us some gold."

———————

Silas doffed his flight suit and depressed the button on the King radio strapped in his chest pack. "Jumper crew, this is Kent. Sound off for par."

He released the button and listened. Half a minute later he stretched his neck from side to side and then repeated the transmission.

Still no answer.

He needed to get to higher ground, evaluate his position and estimate the landing points of the crew. Radio communications might be more effective on a ridgetop anyway. He stowed his jumpsuit at the base of the tree his chute hung in and pulled from it a few useful items—an LED headlamp, a couple carabiners, fuchsia ribbon flagging, some flint, and a pair of soot-stained white leather gloves.

He headed in the direction his crew should have landed. He felt his pulse inside his head, every systolic compression drumming on the inside of his cranium. A smoky haze hovered in his path. The acrid air made his eyes water. Sunlight waned from the forest floor, replaced by shadows and flying insects and the growing din of crickets. How long had he been unconscious in that tree?

The forest ahead began to look just like the forest all around. Silas tore off a piece of flagging and tied it to a fallen log. As he cinched down the knot, something dark and wet dripped onto his hand. Overhead, the canopy stood shadowed, a thick network of branches and limbs. The drip fell again, splashing onto his skin. He stared closer at it. In the fading light he discerned a rusty red color.

Realization soaked in, slow and thick. He stumbled backward, stared again into the canopy, his head spinning with a sense of vertigo. He made out a twisted chute blocking the fading sunlight. Below it hung the twisted form of a smokejumper's body.

"Hey!" Silas waved. "Hey! I see you. Can you hear me? Hang on. I'll find a way to get to you."

The body was a hundred feet up a sequoia that had a trunk as thick as an airplane hull. He had no idea how he could get up there. He searched the immediate area, as if a pair of crampons and climbing gear would suddenly appear. Maybe he could work his rope around the trunk and counterbalance off of it, slowly make his way up. . . . He stared at the tree trunk and the distance up. No way.

"If you can hear me, wave a hand or a foot."

No movement.

No sound.

Another blood drop hit the log beside him.

Silas stretched his fingers across his brow. The path he'd followed to that point blended into black. He strapped his LED light on his head and clicked it on.

No communications. No contact with the rest of the crew. What more could he do here?

He was torn. Night was falling. Continue in the direction of those who jumped before him, or turn around and hike in the direction Jumper 41 went down.

Not counting whoever was in that tree, there were five other jumpers who should be in close proximity of each other. Elle, on the other hand, would be completely alone.

That settled it.

He wrapped the sequoia three times with the bright pink flagging and set off for Crystal Lake.

"I'll be back for you."

Pale blue light diffused over the ground in front of him. He tied off flagging to saplings and manzanita bushes every couple thousand feet, trail markers as he made his way.

Caleb cursed.

Cleese shifted his gaze from the tree canopy to Caleb, his helmet brim shadowing his face from the light strapped to the front of it. "I'd say Monte looks good as dead." He spat. "And I reckon he didn't flag his own tree."

"I've got footprints over here." Rapunzel waved Caleb over. A set of prints tracked onward into the forest, the boot print matching the brand of Whites they all wore.

Caleb ran his hand over his chin. This was not going well.

"How in the—" He cut himself off, fuming with anger. Either Silas had somehow survived his jump or they had unexpected company. He already had one injured crew member and now another was dead.

Refined, a gold brick weighed seventy pounds. Add in the weight of unrefined ore, and they were going to have to move thousands of pounds. He'd secured a Huey, so the weight wouldn't be a problem for transport out. It was getting the gold from the prospector's cache to the helicopter landing zone. *Thanks, Monte.*

Rapunzel mumbled, "Leaves a bigger cut for the rest of us."

Sippi shook his head and stared at the hanging body. "I would have gladly paid Monte to carry his share. God rest his soul."

Rapunzel slapped the back of Sippi's helmet. "Listen to you, talking like a minister. You don't even know what you're say—"

Sippi punched him.

Rapunzel reeled backward, then tackled Sippi at the waist. The two scuffled in the dirt, light beams streaking in wild patterns.

A gunshot fired.

The group froze. Their eyes fixed on Caleb, who stood with his semiautomatic Ruger pointed at the ground.

The smell of gunpowder met Caleb's nostrils. "None of you is of much use to us dead. Now can we focus, please, on our mission? Accomplish this one simple task and you will have enough money to go wherever you want, for as long as you want. If you want to kill each other after we finish our mission, that's your prerogative. But until that gold cache is loaded on a helicopter, we all need each other. That second charge failing to blow has thrown us off course. Now Monte's dead, Bo's hurt, and we all have to carry more than our own share of the weight. That's the way it is. We've got a hike ahead and time working against us. So let's focus and get this done. Is that understood?"

Rapunzel nodded, eyes toward the dirt. Sippi said, "Yeah," and looked away. Bo gave acknowledgement with a subtle nod. Cleese, still behind Caleb, remained just out of peripheral view.

Sippi cracked his neck. "So what do we do with Monte?"

"Nothing. His body will corroborate our story. Plane went down with engine trouble. We made an emergency jump, and it took us several days to establish radio communications with the repeater burned up. Monte's death will make it look legit."

Caleb set the safety on his Ruger and holstered it at the bottom of his pack. "We still need to head a decent way from here. Let's hike on."

––––––––––––

Silas paused in the blackness. Was that a gunshot? He clicked off his helmet light. It had been faint. Distant. What else could it be? A fallen tree? Rock slide? An explosion from Jumper 41?

Crickets chirped. Rodents skittered. Pine needles whispered, swaying in the smoke-scented breeze. And the creek rippled soft, cool as it flowed from the place he was heading.

Stars that would've peeked through the treetops were no longer visible, hidden behind a smoky veil.

The fire wasn't far.

Silas turned on his light and angled his route closer to the creek. He had to focus. Find higher ground and reestablish radio communications. Follow the creek toward Crystal Lake to find Elle. If he could make the ridge bordering Crystal Lake, he could kill two birds with one stone. A vision played in his mind of Elle's plane smashing into a mountainside. He shook his head to clear the thought, forcing instead a picture of her skimming Jumper 41 across the surface of the water and swimming to safety on the shore.

She'd been descending so fast . . .

He'd go crazy if he thought of only that all night. His pace quickened. He needed to slow a bit to conserve energy and avoid any pitfalls in the pitch-black of the forest floor. Who knew what was out there, beyond the radius of his helmet light.

The dark edge blurred reality and possibility. The landscape as he thought it should be became something wrought in the cauldron of his imagination. As such, and in the way that dreams were, subtle details began to shift and twist logic. Before long he found himself in a waking sleep state, too tired to raise his wrist and check the time, too determined to stop and sleep. The substance of his fears and longings formed in the unseen all around.

Elle . . .

Images flooded his mind like the waters of Crystal Lake must have the plane. What was better . . . for her to have died suddenly on impact, or to have borne a tortuous combination of injuries that simply delayed death into the night?

He hoped and prayed, selfishly, that no matter the extent of injuries she might still be alive. That he could see her again and hear her breathe and say the things that needed to be said.

CHAPTER 28

Madison . . .

Elle's daughter consumed her thoughts as the last of the heat left the dark granite slab she lay out on. Diffuse moonlight spread through the smoke-filled sky. Her clothes stuck to her body, the dampness sending chills across her skin with the downslope breeze blowing toward the lake a short walk away.

Would Maddie think she'd forgotten about her? Left her there alone in the hospital? She shook the thought from her mind. Maddie had Carol Weathers. She was in good hands. But still . . .

She tried to think of any scenario in which Silas could have somehow grabbed a parachute before being thrown from the plane. She shook her head, eyes growing hot. She didn't want to think about it. This place was a curse, taking from her the only men she loved.

Yes . . . she couldn't deny it or hide from it. Loved.

She sat up, wiped her eyes, and studied the smoky clouds. Visibility would hamper any immediate rescue efforts. For the next day or two, the best she could hope for was to reunite with the rest of the jumper crew, take an inventory of supplies—find a way to survive. But for the immediate future, she was on her own.

Gone was Jumper 41, along with her survival pack and tools. She had no radio, no food, no shelter. At least it was summer and she had fresh water to drink.

She recalled a childhood memory of once being separated

from her father at a campground. After their evening walk, they'd stopped so he could use the restroom. She heard a skittering from behind what she thought was their friends' camp. She went to inspect it and her flashlight started to cut out. A couple wrong turns and soon she was on an adjacent road. It was a campground loop within a loop. But to her, at nine years old and in the black of the evening, it all looked the same.

Wandering that loop for fifteen minutes, with a dimming incandescent flashlight that she had to shake to keep on, felt like the entire night. She was sure she was lost in a vast wilderness and would never find civilization again. When her father found her she was sobbing and shaking and refused to let go of him until they reached their tent.

Lying on the granite slab, she watched glints of moonlight breaking through a slim crack in the expansive smoke cloud, dancing on the water's surface. The wind carried the scents of burnt timber and foliage. Elle brought her knees to her chest and wrapped her arms around them.

The manzanita below her rock shook and rustled. She held her breath. *That wasn't the wind.* The bushes shook again and a black bear cub toddled out. Her eyes widened. If baby was here that could only mean one thing.

Momma wasn't far behind.

A low rumbling huff sounded to her side. She heard the sound of sniffing and a heavy exhale. The manzanita shook again, though this time it didn't rustle so much as bend and crack. The form of a full-size black bear emerged not ten feet from her.

The animal stopped broadside and turned her large head toward Elle, her face lit by a wash of faint blue. Large, round, and black, the mother bear's eyes fixed on Elle. As the bear exhaled through her snout and huffed, Elle swallowed and worked to recall the things her father had taught her about bears when they hiked. If they saw one, her father had explained, he would raise his arms in the air and make as much noise as possible, trying to look as large as possible, and she should do the same. Black bears usually weren't aggressive, he'd said. Unless it's a mother with her cubs and she feels surprised or threatened.

Elle's instincts cautioned against trying to scare off the bear. She had to hope the mother had picked up Elle's scent a long time ago—had watched her since dusk and decided she wasn't a threat.

The mother huffed again and shook her head before swinging down toward the pond to follow the cub to the shore. Elle watched the bear's massive hindquarters wobble down the bank.

Apparently, Elle didn't come across as dangerous to the bear, a trait at the moment she was thankful for. In the moonlight that reflected dimly off the water, she could make out more detail on the bears. Water dripped from the cub's snout while the mother stood watch. Her ears twitched and shifted with the varied sounds of small forest creatures.

Elle's heart pounded in her chest. She felt both exhilarated and petrified. Her muscles were exhausted. Sleep hung heavy on her eyelids, but she didn't dare shut them. She couldn't risk lying down. Not with the forest alive and shuffling about and a mother bear only fifty feet away.

No. It was going to be a long, long night.

CHAPTER 29

Silas's tongue tasted like dust.

The creek bubbled close by. He worked his way over to it and dipped his hand into the dark water, his headlamp reflection a waving blue orb on the surface. He splashed his face and unscrewed his canteen. Dirt receded in brown streaks across his hands. The sound of conversation filtered through the trees. He rose and squinted in the darkness. Five figures appeared at the edge of the lamplight.

"Hey." He coughed and cleared his throat. "Hey. Over here."

————

Bo shook his head, watching Silas buying off on Caleb's compliments.

"You made it. So glad we found you, brother."

Silas smiled, shook hands, and patted arms.

The pain in Bo's side burned like a brand. He winced and pressed it with his palm to stabilize.

If only that fool spotter had a clue. Little did he know that his walking on terra firma constituted a miracle to these men who'd just tried to kill him. He moved among thieves, liars, and murderers, and there wasn't one of them who didn't want him dead.

A fresh trickle of blood rolled down Bo's flank.

The overlapping headlamp lights produced an artificial moonlight glow among the group. Cleese squatted in the duff, tracing fingers along the edge of his woodsman's knife. Sippi spat tobacco in the stream. Rapunzel leaned against a tree by Silas and Caleb.

Bo sucked a deep breath. He trusted that the Lord had a plan in all this. But it would be one, he feared, that again involved saving the hide of this knuckle-headed white kid.

Bo walked to the creek and crouched to fill his canteens. Erratic winds were already picking up. The smell of smoke stronger.

Down the bank, Caleb squeezed Silas on the shoulder. "Monte's not your fault or mine or anybody else's. The engine failed. We all made the best jump we could. It's a stroke of luck that any of us survived."

Silas shook his head, regret painting his down-turned face. "I can't stop thinking about—"

"Captain Westmore?"

Silas nodded.

"We'll get to her. I'll make sure of it."

Silas glanced over at Bo. He shook his head. "We've got an injured member. It can't be good for him to keep this pace. We should split into teams, one head back to Monte, in case he's still alive."

"He ain't." Cleese sheathed his knife.

Silas turned. "How do you know?"

"I seen his eyes."

Silas swallowed and glanced at Caleb.

Caleb nodded. "Fixed and dilated."

Silas ran a hand over his mouth. "Still. Someone should stay with the body. Bo's the logical choice."

Bo couldn't let them be separated. Silas's good intentions

worked in spite of himself. Bo mustered his best ability to stand upright and appear healthy. "I can hold my own. I ain't leaving you all."

Silas tightened his brow. "And if I give you a direct order?"

"There ain't one of us who's going to get out of this wilderness in less than two days' time. Monte's body is safe where it is. Would you rather leave me, an injured man, alone that long?"

Silas shook his head. "You're right. Okay, but let me know if you can't keep the pace. If we need to split up, we will. Finding Elle is our first priority."

Bo nodded. *Atta boy.*

Silas cleared his throat, drew a composed breath, and addressed the group. "I know we've all been impacted by the loss of Monte. But there's a chance our pilot is still alive. So here it is—our first mission is to locate her and render aid as . . . if, needed. Our second priority is to reestablish communications and get ourselves out of here. Given the condition of our crew and lack of supplies and tools, it's obvious that our former mission of corralling the southern flank of this complex is aborted. Any questions?" He scanned their faces. "Okay. Fill your canteens and pack up. We'll follow the creek toward Crystal Lake where she hoped to land."

The men shifted positions and secured their packs. Bo crouched alongside Silas at the creek.

Bubbles escaped his canteen underwater. "Who said a spare tire was good for nothing?" He gripped a handful of fat on his unwounded side. "Plenty of padding. Few stitches and I'll be fine." He glanced behind him and lowered his voice. "You should know, these boys ain't the forgiving type. You best wake up and realize you is—"

Caleb walked past them, shouldering his pack.

Silas rested on his haunches and dunked a canteen into the creek. He studied Bo, then whispered, "You knew the plane was going down?"

"Yes."

"How?"

"Why is the question."

"And?"

Bo arched his back and looked away. With his index finger he scrawled in the muddy bank.

Gold.

Silas kept his eyes fixed on the dirt.

Bo stood, placed a boot on top of the word and pivoted. Silas let out a breath and screwed the lid on his canteen.

Gray smoke wavered in Bo's headlamp light. The wind snaked past him, carrying the sound of crackling fire upon it.

Still in a crouch, Silas stared at him.

Bo held his gaze and then walked to the end of the crew line. There he clicked off his helmet light, steadied himself against a tree, and sent off a prayer. Moisture broke at the bridge of his nose, the searing iron in his side boring deep.

"All right, boys." Silas stood and turned to the group. "Let's get moving."

CHAPTER 30

Silas tried to convince himself that the discomfort he felt hiking at the front of his crew stemmed from his new role as a spotter, from his unfamiliarity with the guys—the lack of rapport. What did they think of him, of his decisions? Were they on board, eager to follow and to support? Were they begrudging him, judging him?

But he had to be honest. His unvoiced concerns drew from deeper than that. How did Bo know that he would need an emergency backup chute unless Bo knew something was going to happen? Did he know the engine was going to explode? Did they all? Is that why Bo didn't want to talk about it within earshot of the group?

Why in the world would a smokejumper crew sabotage its own plane?

He'd been the new guy before. He'd been the jumper in charge on countless missions. This wasn't just nerves. Something was way off. What and why, though? He just couldn't land a boot on it.

Monte was dead. Rapunzel and Sippi loomed like jackals. Cleese and Caleb walked with grim expressions fixed in their faces.

Caleb hiked directly behind him. Silas shortened his stride, slowing his pace to even up with Caleb. Caleb simply smiled and drew back a step behind. Silas played with his hiking pace, at times slowing to almost a crawl. The entire crew kept behind him.

They wanted him in front.

Where he could be seen.

The muscles in his shoulders tensed. A thousand pine needles poked at his back.

Cleese appeared beside him. "Hey, Spotter."

Breath left his chest. "You startled me."

Cleese spread his lips in a grimacing smile. "Woods'll do that to you at night."

Silas eyed him.

Cleese kept pace. "Saw a wolf once out here."

"In the Desolation Wilderness?"

"I know. Hardly believed it. Thought they'd all hightailed it north." He spat. "We all seen black bears and mountain lions. But a wolf. There's a real killer. Something special."

Silas's heart hammered. He unscrewed his canteen lid and wetted his throat.

Cleese cracked his neck. "People never much liked the wolf. Too cunning for them. One moment a guy might be strolling along, next moment he's dead. Killed by a wolf smarter than he is."

Silas stopped and faced him. "Fascinating Mutual of Omaha narrative, Cleese. But you know what? My mind is on a dozen different things right now. So why don't you do this—Back. Off."

Cleese seethed with eyes like charcoal briquettes. He cracked his neck again, spat near Silas's feet, and fell back in line.

Silas strode forward, sweat beading at his temples. He glanced back. No one made eye contact.

No one, except for Bo. He trailed in the rear, a story in his face deeper than the wound in his side.

———

Caleb insisted on bedding down for a brief rest around three A.M. The smell of smoke thickened, and the popping and sparking of wood became a constant background din. Silas made out faint red glows on hillsides. There was no way these guys would actually want to take a nap with the fire looming like it was. Thanks to Bo, he was under no illusions. None of them intended to sleep.

Letting the group think that he was unaware gave him the advantage of surprise. But that was it. The thick smoke screen overhead obliterated any moonlight. Once the headlamps were out, any one of them could sneak up in the dark.

Silas trudged over to a large boulder and slumped down beside it. A few feet away, Bo set his Pulaski against the edge of the rock, along with his pack. As he knelt to tie a boot string, his eyes flashed up to Silas, over to the Pulaski, and back to Silas. He stood and shuffled over to a log just beyond his pack and leaned back, tilting his helmet forward.

The firm boulder felt good to put his weight against. He clicked off his headlamp and watched as every other light snapped off within minutes. The six of them lay in complete blackness. Silas couldn't see his hand a foot in front of his face.

A collection of images took shape in his mind, a slideshow of events leading up to that moment. Pendleton's death. Was it really the fire that overtook him? The engine explosion. The look on Elle's face when he said he wouldn't leave her.

Minutes stretched on. Every forest-floor skitter made his muscles tense. He tried to control his breathing, tried to stay as still and quiet as possible.

If they wanted him dead, this would be their next chance to strike.

Silas leaned to his side, tracing his hand along the dirt until he found the handle of Bo's Pulaski. He lifted it in silence and brought it in front of him. He shifted his boots beneath him so he rested on his haunches. The scents of damp hummus and muddy banks and dust and sweat and the hanging woodsmoke all met his nostrils. Once he quieted himself, the forest seemed loud—pine-needled branches swaying with the wind, nocturnal creatures scampering about, the rolling babble of the brook. His palms sweated against the wooden axe handle.

He blinked, unable to tell the difference between the back of his eyelids and the space in front of him.

CHAPTER 31

Kent!"

Silas clicked on his headlamp.

Cleese appeared, knife in hand. He swung at Silas's chest.

Silas parried with the Pulaski and rolled to the side. Cleese twisted off balance. Silas swung toward his ankles and connected, sweeping him into the air. Cleese struck the ground hard and flat. Silas stomped the knife hand and raised the axe in the air.

"You trying to kill me, Cleese?" Adrenaline-charged fear pulsed in his veins. "You trying to kill me?"

No eyes were visible beneath the man's shadowed brow, only sudden wrinkles at the edges. A branch snapped. Silas turned and a shoulder collided into his chest, sending him flying. He kept his grip on the axe, pushed up off the ground, and took a punishing fist blow to the face. He turned away, scrambling beneath blows. He clicked off his light. Blue neon streaked in his vision. The attacker groped wildly, landing a hand on his neck. He grabbed hold and beat the back of Silas's head and face. Silas tucked his chin, gripped the head of his Pulaski, and drove the handle backwards. It connected with flesh, producing a deflating grunt. Silas repeated the move again and again, like a piston. The last drive sounded and felt like it cracked a rib in the assailant.

The body behind him slumped to the ground, and Silas made

his feet, chest heaving. He tried to swallow against a parched throat. His heart pounded against his sternum.

Ten feet away, a helmet light clicked on, silhouetting the form beneath it and revealing Rapunzel doubled over on the ground beside Silas.

Caleb spoke, "Go ahead and turn on your light, Kent. I want to be sure you know your predicament."

Silas clicked on his headlamp, illuminating Caleb's anterior and revealing Cleese, who stood beside him, knife once again in hand.

A shadow moved behind Silas. Sippi punched him in the flank and wrapped his arm around Silas's neck. Silas maneuvered and writhed, but Sippi squeezed tight.

His vision blackened at the edges. His lungs ached for air.

"Give it up, Spotter." Sippi wrenched the sleeper hold tighter. "Give it up before you give out."

Voices muffled. Images blurred. Cleese separated into two men, spinning knives in their palms.

Caleb cross-dissolved into triplicate and back. He extended a hand toward Cleese. His voice came from a distant cavern. "Now give me my Ruger, and let's be done with it."

"Get your own gun."

The arteries in Silas's head swished slow, heavy blood. His legs buckled. His vision narrowed to a pinhead of light.

"Don't play with me, Cleese. It ain't in my pack. What did you do with it?"

"I didn't do—"

A pistol hammer cocked.

A deep, slow voice spoke from the shadows, "Let the spotter go."

The vise on his windpipe released. Silas sucked a breath and fell to his knees. He coughed and gasped and rubbed his throat. He blinked through watering eyes to see Bo with a handgun barrel rested against Cleese's temple.

"Now, drop the knife."

It fell against the duff with a dull thud.

Silas staggered to his feet, triangulating his position between Sippi and Caleb. Nobody moved, and all was silent until Caleb blew air between his lips and let out a laugh.

"Or what, Bo? Really?" He stepped forward, away from Cleese and Bo, the light from his helmet moving with him. He stared at Silas, shoulders relaxed. "I think you and I both know that Bo isn't going to pull that—"

A shot burst.

Caleb thrust his hands up. Sippi ducked. Silas froze in a semisquat, unable to see Cleese behind Caleb.

Bo shouted, "Put your hands on your head and your heads in the dirt. To your knees. Now."

Caleb, Sippi, and Rapunzel all complied. Bo dragged Cleese's limp body behind a tree.

Caleb cursed.

Bo emerged. "Silas, get my pack."

Silas hesitated but read a beckoning in Bo's expression. Silas found Bo's pack and shouldered it.

Bo came alongside him, pistol trained on the kneeling men. "Cut some parachute cord and tie their hands and feet. Any y'all fools move, and you going to face the same fate as Cleese."

Silas dropped the packs away from the group and pulled a bind of p-cord from a pouch. He cinched down tight knots, securing each man's ankles and wrists behind them, keeping their foreheads propped in the dirt. He took the pocketknives and multi-tools the men had on their persons, searched their packs for more of the same, and then went back to search for the knife in the area where Cleese had been standing.

His headlamp traced the ground, circling.

A dust-covered blade caught his eye. Silas crouched to pick it up and scanned the area where Cleese had been standing.

Strange. No blood.

"Let's get going, Spotter."

Silas hoisted Bo's pack and followed him away from the scene, deep into the trees, across the creek, and into the gullet of the night.

CHAPTER 32

Bo spoke little. He led by compass in the direction of Crystal Lake, seeing in Silas a tenuous trust that brimmed with questions.

His eyes became accustomed to traveling through the night, picking up the rimmed red glow of the fire's progress down hillsides. The first peek of dawn crept through the evergreen curtains after a couple hours of hiking. The forms of knee-high boulders and the edges of shrubs and trees washed into better view. By Bo's estimation, they'd put a decent four to five miles between them and Caleb's crew.

He worked his way down toward a dry creek bed, crossed over it, and started up the opposite hillside. Caleb's pistol rubbed a sore spot in the small of his back. He stopped when he realized Silas was no longer behind him.

Silas stood on the other side of the draw, pack on his shoulders and Pulaski in hand. He stared at Bo. "You didn't have to kill him."

Bo took a seat in the dirt, pulled the gun from his belt, and drew his knees up. "How's that now?"

"Cleese. You didn't have to shoot the guy in the head."

Bo sniffed. "And what do you suggest I should have done?"

"I don't know. Anything. Something else."

"And how is it you know I shot him in the head?"

"I heard it. I saw . . ."

"Did you?"

"I saw you drag his body behind the tree."

"And how did I drag him?"

"Your arms. They were around his . . . around his neck." Silas's face relaxed. "You choked him out, didn't you."

"Mm-hmm." Bo smiled. "Dead, no. Unconscious, yes."

Silas searched the creek bank as if he was watching it all unfold in his head.

Bo swatted at a mosquito. "I'll admit . . . I did shoot the fool in the foot though."

Sweat trickled behind Bo's ears. The searing in his side refused to let up. Struggling with Cleese and then dragging him behind that tree had taken more out of him than he'd expected.

Silas exhaled and leaned on the Pulaski. "I didn't tie him up. I thought he was shot in the head."

"S'all right. I had some spare p-cord in my pants pocket. It's enough to buy us some time."

Silas straightened and scanned the terrain behind them. "You think they're on our tail already?"

Bo took a deep breath. "Probably. They're determined. They know we want to find our pilot, but they've also got a timetable to keep. I imagine they'll split up and send a couple guys after you and me."

Silas shook his head. "What did you mean when you wrote *Gold* in the dirt?"

"They're on a mission. The plane engine. Your chutes. The confrontation last night. You done used up most of your smoke-jumper lives on this one."

"My chutes?"

"They sliced them up good when you was in the cockpit with the pilot. I figured you'd notice."

"The timing of my exit was . . . unexpected. The emergency chute you gave me was all I had. I never thanked you."

Bo tipped his head.

"What do you know about this gold they're after?"

"You heard of the Independence Find?"

Silas nodded.

"They done found it."

Silas ran a hand behind his neck. "People have been . . . How?"

"Caleb got GPS coordinates from Chief Shivner. Couple years ago Shivner discovered a hidden bunker with the gold by accident. But he didn't have the means to extract the find. He saw an opportunity with the fire and enlisted Caleb to do the dirty work."

"And Pendleton's death?"

"Murder. After Caleb confirmed the location of the bunker, there was a ruckus with an old man with a shotgun who was trying to protect the gold. Pendleton got in the middle of it and protested. Cleese jumped the old man and the weapon fired, killing Pendleton. The old man tried to get away, and Cleese shot him as well. They dumped the bodies in the bunker and concocted a story about being burned over to cover up Pendleton's death."

"Sounds like their timetable to get back to that bunker has as much to do with erasing evidence as it does recovering the gold."

"And now erasing evidence involves erasing us."

"Why didn't you tell someone when you got back?"

Bo stared at the ground. "Maybe I should have. But it wasn't that easy."

"Why?"

"Caleb threatened my sisters." Images of Jamal on the

sidewalk flashed through his mind. Bo shook his head. "They the last family I have. He knows what college they go to. Where they live." Bo stood and dusted off his pants. "We best keep moving."

"I know there's little chance Elle survived. If we continue on for that lake, they might intercept us."

"Think of it this way—if Captain Westmore is alive and they find her—"

"She'd think they came to help. She'd be captured."

Bo cleared his throat. "Or worse."

Silas stepped across the rocky creek bed. "About two, three miles now, you think?"

Bo brought a hand to his side and sucked air through his teeth. "Sounds about right."

"You going to be able to make it?"

"Sure. Sure."

"Make sure you drink enough."

"Hold this." Bo handed him the gun and pulled out his canteen. He shook the nearly empty bottle and tipped the last trickle of water into his mouth.

Silas offered his canteen, and Bo poured a little from it into his.

"Give yourself more."

He did so and handed it back to Silas. "Thank you."

Silas took a swig and slid the canteen back in its pouch. He offered the pistol back to Bo.

Bo waved a hand. "You hang on to it."

Silas cinched it into the pouch beside the water bottle and started up the hill. "If anyone could've put that plane down and survived, it's Elle."

CHAPTER 33

Elle fought the serotonin urge to wake with the glow outside her eyelids. But morning had come—and with it welcome warmth and the slogging feeling of little sleep. She sat up on the boulder, arching her back and stretching her shoulders, searching for a way to relieve the kinks and soreness that accompanied her evening upon exposed granite.

The sun rose, dressed in smoke, casting an otherworldly amber hue. She slid off the rock, her shoes landing atop large bear paw prints in the dust. She scanned the immediate area, reminded of her nocturnal visitors. If she hadn't felt the urgent need to relieve herself, she likely would have remained on the rock for another hour to ensure they were gone. But nature was calling, and so she circled the boulder to find a reasonable spot.

She walked down to the lake's edge to rinse her hands. Her head pounded when she leaned forward. She lifted her hand to her brow, returning with spotted blood on her fingers. The water rippled with a building breeze. No sight of Jumper 41 remained, leaving her nothing she could salvage. No supplies, no radios, no rations.

Elle's stomach twisted and grumbled. She needed food. Ridges bordered the lake, giving the oversized pond a basin shape. Reasoning that the best way to get fed was to get found, she retraced her headings before putting the Twin Otter down.

She'd flown in from the north and east. She oriented herself halfway between the flight path in and the rising sun.

That's my way home.

It was one thing to backpack on an established route. Another to trail blaze through dense forest and over rocky terrain with no food in her system. She checked all her pockets, feeling in the small coin pocket of her pants something like a folded paper. Elle threaded her fingers in and felt the soft texture of a leaf. She lifted it to her nose and inhaled the scent of mint. Visions of Silas flooded her mind. She bit off a part of the leaf and sucked on it to make it last. It took her mind off of the hunger but made her heart ache.

She wiped her eyes. She needed to stay focused.

If she stuck to a northeasterly route, there was a chance she'd come across her jumper crew. The wind kicked up, swaying branches in erratic patterns. The sky overhead darkened and rumbled. Elle wove between manzanita bushes and skirted along the narrow shore of the lake. The farther she could get while she still had energy reserves, the better.

A piece of shale broke off in her hand. She tossed it to the side and found a better handhold, pulling herself up to the ridge crest. The strong breeze cooled her skin through the portions of her clothes that were still damp from the day before. The terrain stretched out beyond with its rocky crags and undisturbed evergreen stands.

Strange seeing the familiar landscape again, but on foot this time.

She had flown over so many square miles of the Desolation

Wilderness during the three long weeks searching for her father. Taxing her child-care resources, Elle took only the minimum breaks required by the FAA for sleep, and then she was back in the cockpit the minute she was eligible to fly. Exactly twenty-one days, and the last was the worst.

Turbulent, to say the least. The ground and sky married in mixed grays. The scattered wildlife she'd seen so often during prior flights—deer, antelope, coyotes, black bears—were nowhere to be seen. As though they knew a storm was coming. The berries and nuts they'd squirreled away to that point would have to suffice.

Snow was coming.

The National Weather Service had forecasted significant amounts of snow over the next week, as much as four feet overnight. Tower had advised against the flight. The Forest Service almost forbade her from further use of the aircraft. But Weathers stood in the gap, using all his weight to give her a green light for one last mission.

One last chance to find her dad.

During the first few days after his plane went missing, she'd flown directly over what she believed were his charted flight-route options. When those efforts produced nothing, she expanded her search of the Desolation Wilderness and spiraled out in an expanding orbit. Again, when the search came up empty, she elected to begin a comprehensive search method, thoroughly covering every topographic square on her map, beginning with her best guesstimates and crossing them off, one by one.

She remembered sitting in the cockpit that last day, the aircraft still on the tarmac. Rain flicked across the windshields. Wind shook the hull. She held the Desolation map in front of her. One hundred and sixty square miles, and she'd only comprehensively covered seventy of them. The first week she had tons of help. Everything from public agencies to private aviators and friends of her dad. But as the fourteenth day came around without any sign of her father's aircraft, the passion to search waned, much like the media coverage surrounding his disappearance. Elle soon found herself as the lone pilot left.

"It's just a recovery effort now, Elle."

"You can't keep up this pace. This isn't a rescue mission anymore."

"It's time to accept that he's gone."

As she sat in the plane, preparing to take off, she'd traced her hand along the map. Creases and indentations scattered across it from the persistent checking and marking. She followed with her fingertips the red line marking her father's last known flight path from the South Lake Tahoe airport. The line halted a portion of the way into the Desolation, the time of his last report to the tower.

What happened, Dad?

The weather had been clear the day he flew. Crisp, autumnal. The forest floor colored with the yellows, reds, and oranges of changing aspens and oaks that traced the mountain streams winding their way through the wilderness.

No lightning. No rain or snow. Winds were calm.

Had to be mechanical failure.

Dad was as diligent as any pilot she'd ever met when it came to preflight checks and preventative maintenance. He knew that Cessna in and out. Still, an old plane was an old plane. A sudden, unexpected mechanical failure could have put him in a tight spot really fast.

Elle used to chide him. "Vintage is great for old cars, Dad. Not for things that leave the ground."

That final day on the runway, she circled her finger on the map around the end of the red line. What options would an engine failure leave him?

Lord, show me.

She studied the topo lines and the elevation markings. The terrain lifted from the paper in her mind. She imagined herself in the cockpit of his Cessna, seeing the lay of the land from a horizontal viewpoint and at a lower altitude than she could safely fly over it. She descended into a canyon and a small clearing opened to her ten o'clock. The narrowest notch the forest could possibly allow a pilot to limp in an aircraft and still walk away.

She blinked, her vision returning to the map in front of her.

Why hadn't she seen it before? She'd flown over the area numerous times, but this tiny clearing, surrounded by craggy cliffs, insignificant enough to be easily missed from high in the air, now became clear when perceived from an imagined lower altitude—the altitude at which a pilot with engine trouble may have been forced to fly. She tapped the spot and nodded. It was her best, last shot.

Thunder rumbled. Elle rolled up the map and switched on the plane's batteries. Lights and indicators glowed. She fired up the engines with a striking whine that fluttered into a chopping roar. She strapped her headset on and clicked the transmit button.

"Tower, Jumper 41 requesting taxi to runway one for takeoff."

The rain turned slushy as she left the ground in South Lake. Static littered radio transmissions, the ridgetop repeaters already feeling the beginnings of the blizzard.

Elle relied on instruments and her knowledge of the heights and shapes of surrounding peaks, adjusting course according to the magnetic compass on the dash to keep on track with her father's route. She skimmed the Twin Otter beneath the cloud cover, threading through canyons and chancing the lower altitude to come upon the point she'd seen in her head. The fog and rain fell thick, but the terrain emerged steadily, a granite-lined corridor, just as she'd pictured it. Somewhere at her ten o'clock, behind a blanket of swirling gray, there should be the small clearing.

She angled toward it. Thunder broke, this time close and violent. Pattering rain morphed into a hailstone barrage. Ice pelted the hull like gravel. Elle dropped altitude with no improvement, canyon sides and treetops now dangerously close. The lead-colored horizon blurred the line between ground and air, moisture seeming to rise from below as much as fall from above. Hot moisture blurred her eyes.

Dad.

Lightning flashed. Thunder rattled the plane. The location of the clearing grew further enshrouded. The storm pressed in, but she held her course. Moisture rolled down her cheeks. If she didn't pull out soon, she'd be flying blind.

She set her jaw with stiff-lipped resolve, angling the yoke hard and swinging the Twin Otter around. She dove lower, weaving between jutting granite and towering sequoias. Tears flowed from her eyes. Sobs interspersed with mechanical movements from throttle to yoke. Visibility approached zero.

This was good-bye.

She pulled back on the yoke and climbed into the cloud cover.

The Desolation swallowed him. Winter had come.

———

A rainbow stretched in a circle between her lashes. Elle blinked twice, reverting her focus to the day at hand. The smell of burning wood dominated the air, the sky filled with smoke-formed thunderheads. She trudged upslope, small dust clouds rising beside her, eager to reach the peak of the hill she was on to attain a new vantage on her progress. Perhaps she would see the crew.

She hadn't given up on finding her father after the last search flight that fall. She'd waited for the spring snowmelt, and when the creeks and rivers swelled, and the last bulk of the snow disappeared, she flew over the location she'd sought that last day of the search.

The clearing was there, just as she suspected. It was big enough to land a plane in an emergency, just as she'd imagined. And it was also completely and serenely untouched and undisturbed, without any sign of a crash or touchdown.

She resigned herself to her friends' admonitions. She needed to move on. Regardless of the fact that no wreckage was found, she needed to "bury" him, to push aside the razor-edged fragments of his Cessna from her mind.

Elle flew back into South Lake that day knowing she needed to close the book on the search. There weren't any tears that time. Only a stoic and stubborn acceptance that some things in life just weren't fair.

Her lungs burned with the present effort of her hill climb. She propped both hands on her knees. Sweat dripped from her nose, coloring the dirt. Almost to the crest. She straightened, hiked to the hilltop, and a grand view opened before her—a verdant, sequoia-filled canyon bordered by granite and a smoky ceiling.

She knew this place.

Never from the ground, but she knew it.

Along the side of the canyon, at the place that would be at

the ten o'clock of an airplane flying in from the opposite side, there branched like a tributary a small clearing nestled in the woods and enclosed by rocky walls.

Dad.

Something rent inside her, like a curtain separating hurt from hope. She shuffled down the hillside, soon leaping over stones and past bushes.

What was she doing? She'd put this behind her.

She shoved past trees. A branch scratched her neck. She pushed on, hurtling stones, clambering over boulders and weaving through the forest. Her route led her downhill, aiding the speed of her progress. Her jogging lagged into a stride and her stride into a hands-on-hips pacing. She fell to her knees in the mud by a stream. Her chest heaved for oxygen. She washed her neck wound and splashed the liquid across her burning cheeks, watching the water fall.

She lifted her head, cool drops tracing down her face. Beyond the opposite bank, sunlight reflected off a jagged piece of fin-sized white metal protruding from the dirt.

Elle rose. She stepped through the creek without taking her eyes off the object. Scores charred its top edge. Painted numbers lay across its face, veiled by the soil. Her hands trembled. She knelt and pulled on it. Fissures etched in the dirt around it. She shook the metal and yanked it from the ground. Dust fell from its sides. She brought it to her lap, wiped away the debris and froze when her hand swiped clear the marking—*N288.*

CHAPTER 34

Tears streamed down Elle's face.

He never made the clearing.

She clutched the vertical fin to her chest and squeezed shut her eyelids, shoulders heaving.

The metal felt cold and grimy. A chill traveled up her arm to her core. She quieted, jaw quivering, and rose. She climbed a craggy route to a vantage point. Along one end of the clearing, sheltered beneath a rock outcropping, she spotted what appeared to be the rest of the tail section.

She drew a deep breath.

The smoky sky muted the light, turning clouds different shades of graphite. Stones tumbled off her feet. She wove her way toward shaded the location of the plane.

It's why she never saw it. It lay hidden. Sheltered. Entombed.

What remained of the hull became visible. Scorched, dirt and moss covered. The nose of the plane lay mashed against the cliff wall. The wings were missing, likely sheered off in the landing. She navigated the uneven ground leading to it, came beside the hull and reached out her hand. It, too, felt cold. Her eyes trailed over the wreckage, over the plane she'd spent countless hours searching for. The plane that held her father.

Her stomach turned. She doubled over and retched upon the ground.

She coughed and spat and ran the back of her hand across

her lips. Her eyes turned toward the front of the plane. Toward what remained of the cockpit. Her stomach flip-flopped.

Elle balanced herself with her free hand on the aircraft and worked her way to the cockpit. The windows were blackened and warped. The mangled door hung outward on the one remaining hinge. She leaned inside, making out melted gauges and vaguely recognizable levers.

No evidence of a pilot. No clothing. No body. Just heaps of ash and char.

Elle straightened. She didn't need to be here anymore.

She didn't know what she had hoped to find. Perhaps just something personal. She looked at the fractured tailpiece in her hand. Something more than just a piece of steel with her father's aircraft markings on it.

She turned to leave, but a glint caught her eye. Amid all the dull black char in the cockpit one tiny object vied for attention. The light caught it again. Elle bent close and reached out for it. Her fingers found a curved piece of metal. The ash fell away, revealing a ring. A platinum wedding band.

The one her father had always worn—even long after her mother had died.

With a quick rub of her thumb she wiped clean the inside of the loop, bringing into view the engraved numbers inside of it.

Their wedding anniversary.

Elle clutched it in her palm. She leaned back into the cockpit and gently swept aside the piles of ash on the floor. She soon saw what she both hoped and feared she would find.

Her father's remains.

She held the ring in a fist to her mouth. Her chest convulsed. She fought the sobs, heavy and labored.

After all her searching, all the tireless flying and searching . . .
She had to crash to find him.

———————

The diffuse sunlight painted half of the canyon a greenish
gold.

Elle heaved another rock onto the makeshift grave. Unwill-
ing to let his skeleton remain on the floor of that cockpit, she
had grimaced through the work of handling her father's remains.
She'd gathered every bone she could find, cradled them, and set
them together, not in order or aligned, but in a pile, as though
his essence somehow inhabited the fragments when they were
congregated.

The knowledge of closure carried her. The ability to act
empowered her, giving her the strength to do what needed to
be done.

With the final rock in place, she set the broken tail fin
between two stones at the head. She took several steps back and
wiped her soil-stained brow.

She pulled her necklace out from her shirt. Her father's ring
now dangled beside the silver cross on it. Farther down the canyon, a whippoorwill let out its cry. A fitting dirge. Elle nodded
and stared at the grave.

She bent to the ground and pinched soil between her fingers.

"Lord, bless him and keep him. Thank you for letting me
find him. For letting me live." She tossed the dirt over the rock
pile. "Dust to dust." She brushed her hands, and let out a breath.

A gun hammer cocked.

Elle spun around, heart racing. She stared into the wrinkled
gray eyes of a whiskered old man, a double-barrel shotgun leveled

her way. A set of blood-stained denim overalls hung from his bony shoulders. His ribs strained with each breath. He hacked a wheezy cough and bared an incomplete set of lower teeth.

"Evening, honey. Fancy finding you here."

CHAPTER 35

Silas overlooked Crystal Lake from the ridgeline. A low smoky ceiling filtered the daylight. Bo stood beside him, the scent of soot strong in the air.

The wind flashed ripples at the water's surface, refracting wheat and amber hues.

No sign of the plane.

No sign of Elle.

He didn't know what he expected to see. His energies and emotions and entire drive from the moment he watched her plane disappear had been focused on finding her. He needed something. Anything.

Bo drew a deep, pensive breath. Perspiration dotted his temples. He pointed off in the distance. "You can't see it with this smoke, but past that ridge there's a draw where the gold bunker is."

"Think they've made it there yet?"

"It's only a matter of time." He drew a pained breath. "Look." He nodded to a tall splintered evergreen halfway down the hill.

Silas sighted it and descended the slope, weaving through thickets and digging his heels into deep duff. He dug his fingers into the bark of a tree trunk and let the cloud of dust around him settle. He glanced up at the broken tree above.

Bo approached, breathing heavily, and licked his lips. "We don't know if she caused that."

Silas scanned the forest floor.

"Maybe she set her down beyond here."

Silas shook his head. "No. This was her best chance. Her only chance."

"If that's true, then Jumper 41 had to've—"

"Sank." Even as he said the word, Silas wished he hadn't. But it wasn't a secret. It was the obvious deduction. "I've got to get closer."

"Why?"

"To see."

"See . . . what, Silas?"

"If she survived the landing. If she did, then maybe she made it to shore. If she made it to shore, then there should be some kind of evidence. Footprints. A fire pit. I don't know. Something."

Bo pressed his bottom lip up, eyes solemn. "All right."

"I saw a slab of granite about midslope over the lake."

"I seen it."

"Should give a decent view of the shoreline."

They wound farther down through manzanita and juniper bushes. Silas used protruding roots as handrails, burying his boots into the mountain to form step shapes for Bo right behind him. They reached the granite ledge. It protruded from the hillside like a vintage Chrysler hood ornament.

Silas dropped Bo's pack where the dirt met the stone. He walked to the edge. It hung out over the water, the lake still far below, expanding out in parabolic perspective.

He studied the perimeter. Marshy reeds bordered the near left bank, thinning out about midway, revealing what appeared to be a decomposing deer carcass along the water's edge. Its antlers looked sawn off, likely poached.

His eyes traced the near edge and followed across to the right. A host of midsized bushes surrounded a grouping of large flat rocks. Beyond that the trees towered toward the top of the basin.

The wind lessened. The water below looked dark and empty, transitioning in depth from a deep blue-green to a darkening plum. He searched for any indication of the aircraft.

Nothing but shadows and flickers.

————

Bo respected Silas's need to grieve. He understood what it meant to be able to have closure. Silas needed that, right then and there, so the haunting *what if*s would not plague the man for years to come.

He decided to give the man some room. He wasn't quite sure just how close Silas and the pilot were, but he suspected they were more than just acquaintances.

Bo stepped around a batch of pine saplings stretching from the dirt along the edge of the granite outcropping and walked along the hillside. A small game trail gave him footing over to a stand of aspens. Behind a larger one he paused to relieve himself.

A collision of thoughts occurred in Bo's head. They'd let down their guard since reaching the lake. He knew he had held Silas's pace back a bit. Last night's struggle had taken more from Bo than he wanted to admit. Their hike had taken too long. He thought of the pistol resting in the pack. He shouldn't have walked away from it. One of them should keep it on their person.

Bo set back toward the rock outcropping. He resolved not to be as sloppy in the future. They needed to keep vigilant. He said a quick prayer beneath his breath, "Lord, give me eyes to see how to save us from this—"

He halted in the patchy cover of the sapling stand. At the base of the granite, where their pack had been dropped, Sippi stood, arm outstretched with the pistol pointed at Silas's back.

Bo was closer to Silas than he was to Sippi. He shouted.

Sippi swung the weapon toward him and fired. Bark splintered. Silas spun, shock in his face. Sippi returned his aim to Silas.

Bo leapt from the tree cover and barreled into Silas.

Silas grunted with the tackle. His feet left the rock. Another gunshot fired. He felt wind and a sudden water impact.

A cocoon of bubbles surrounded them.

Bo's grip weakened. Silas felt warmth across his palm on Bo's back. The water swirled crimson.

He tightened an arm around Bo and kicked for the air. He broke the choppy surface and gasped for breath, water slapping them in the cheeks.

No sign of Sippi on the rock outcropping. His boots weighted him like anchors. Bo's head nodded forward. Silas swirled his legs to tread water, quadriceps burning and lungs taxed.

He lifted Bo's head. The man's eyes drooped, scant breath moving through his parted lips. Blood seeped through the front of his shirt. Silas held pressure on the wound. "Bo!"

Bo blinked and focused.

"You're shot, Bo."

Bo's mouth moved.

Silas brought his ear to Bo's mouth.

The voice was strained. "You got to help my sisters."

Silas scanned the hillside again. "You can help them yourself."

They had to get out of sight.

Bo grabbed the back of Silas's neck and leaned his forehead against him. "My sis—My sisters."

"Okay. Yes. Yes, I will. We will."

Bo coughed in a fit. Pink, frothy sputum oozed from his mouth.

Silas pulled for the shore. "Hang in there, buddy. Hang in there."

Bo hacked again, blood trickling to his chin. "Silas . . ."

Silas kept paddling. "We've got to get clear of here."

"Sil—" His head fell to the water.

Silas propped it back up and slapped his cheek. "Come on, Bo. Stay awake."

Bo opened his eyes and found Silas. He fought back a coughing fit. "My treasure—" He hacked.

"You're not part of that, Bo. Come on. I'll get us to shore."

"No." He squeezed Silas's shoulder.

Silas stared at him.

"My treasure—" He sucked a breath. "My treasure . . . ain't here."

His grip loosened.

"Bo?"

Bo's eyes dilated.

"Bo."

A shot fired, splashing in the water near them. Sippi plunged down the hillside below the outcropping.

Silas gulped air and pulled Bo under. They dipped below as gunshots echoed, thrusting bullets through the water in long thin spears.

Silas struggled for depth, yanking Bo downward.

The water grew murky. Everything fell quiet, cold and still.

He pulled Bo close. Bo's eyes were still open, pupils fixed and unreactive. Silas felt for a pulse on Bo's neck.

Nothing.

He checked again, repositioning his fingertips.

No heartbeat.

His lungs burned. He glanced at the wavy gray-lit surface. The moment they surfaced, Sippi would shoot.

He stared again into Bo's pupils.

You can see when their soul has left them . . .

Silas trembled. He put a hand across Bo's heart, swallowed the last of the air in his cheeks, and pushed the heroic man's body toward the surface.

Forgive me.

Bo ascended in a sanguine cloud.

Silas pulled himself sideways, swimming as fast and as far as he could, fighting the urge to breathe in the water around him. He stroked and kicked until he reached as safe a distance as he could bear. The water grew muddy and tangled with draping roots and algae. He surfaced in a bed of cattails and drew several breaths.

His head spun with lightness, but he took another fresh breath and slipped below, navigating the thicket of water reeds. He rose to the surface again and examined the immediate surroundings. He slowly exhaled. The reeds waved around him, and about thirty yards away by the shore below the granite outcropping, Sippi stood knee-deep in the water, his gun pointed at Bo's surfaced body.

A scarlet sun flared across Silas's yellow fire shirt at the right chest—the mirrored side of the gunshot that had gone through Bo's chest. The muscle beneath felt tender. A quick look revealed a nasty purple bruise but no broken skin.

A wave of grief washed over him. He pushed it from his mind, damming up his feelings. He needed to survive.

To think clearly.

Act decisively.

He'd blend in better with just the dark blue T-shirt he wore beneath his yellow fire shirt. Through the reeds he kept his eyes fixed on Sippi and undid the large buttons. He stripped the shirt off of his shoulders and rolled it into a bundle, holding it in one hand beneath the water's surface.

Sippi looked behind himself and uphill. Silas heard faint conversation, but nothing discernable. Sippi kept one hand on the pistol and with the other waved. Midslope, on the opposite side of the granite outcropping, Rapunzel appeared, lumbering along and favoring his injured flank, working his way down through the ground cover.

Silas searched his surroundings. He wouldn't be safe in the water for long. They likely didn't know if he was shot and floating just beneath the surface or if he had made it to the shore. No doubt they would soon search the banks.

He remembered the animal carcass along the shore. About twenty feet from him now, down the bank in the opposite direction from Sippi lay the rotting deer he'd seen when he and Bo first descended into the lake basin.

Silas lifted his shirt from the water. A plan birthed in his mind. He took another look at Sippi. Rapunzel neared the shore next to him.

The light breeze over the lake proved opportune. Silas could move with stealth and not create a revealing wake. He took a couple minutes to move the short distance, not wanting to chance alerting the duo with the sound of his motion. He came upon the carcass, decomposing and fly infested on the shore. The water there was thicker and greener than near the reed stand, which still served to hide him from Sippi and Rapunzel's view. Unfortunately, he also could no longer see them.

Silas tried to breathe through his mouth. The stench of the animal hovered thick; the cloud of insects pelted his face. He turned away, drew a deep breath, and firmed his resolve. He unraveled his yellow shirt, tied a sleeve to each of the deer's front legs, and draped the rest over the animal's torso. Shooting a glance back down the shore, he exhaled, buried his face in his shoulder, and sucked in another breath. As quietly as he could, he dragged the beast into the water.

At first it began to sink, then, as if equalizing, it found a balance point a couple feet under the surface.

Perfect.

Silas escorted it out deeper, to the edge of the reed blind, and gave it a final shove toward the center of the lake.

He waded low back to the beach, slime coating his neck, flies flitting about his head, landing in his hair and on his ears. At the shoreline he crept low, army style, moving only to a crouch once he was a decent fifty feet into the forest. The ground edged upward, and soon he was half-hiking, half-climbing the basin hillside, working his way with adrenaline-fueled liberation up and away from the lake, from the place of Elle's crashing and the site of Bo's sacrifice.

He emerged from the trees and saw the ridgeline within a stone's throw. Breathing hard, he worked his way up hand over hand along a jagged rock face until he crested the hill. He crouched low beside the rock wall and spotted Sippi on the opposite side of the lake from where he'd set out the deer carcass.

Less than fifty feet away Rapunzel lumbered, a hand around the cracked ribs courtesy of Silas last night. He no doubt desired to stay close to the man with the gun. Sippi shouted to him and pointed across the lake. His focus was not high toward Silas's position but down at the level of the water. Silas followed the direction of Sippi's pointing. One-third of the way out from the shore nearest to him floated a dark form with a waving yellow shirt.

The ruse had worked—for the moment. It would buy Silas the time to get out of the lake basin. But probably not much more. The thick mud on the lakeside was replete with his prints. They'd no doubt soon recognize that the form in the water was not his.

Fifteen minutes. Maybe twenty.

But the smoke was thickening and he had a jump on them, no matter how slim.

CHAPTER 36

Git."

Elle translated the old man's slang. *Keep moving.* She wove in front of him along a narrow trail that led out of the gully and deeper into the forest. A solid ninety-degree detour from the way she wanted to be going.

All she wanted now was to get back to Maddie.

Could things get more bizarre? She always checked her aircraft engines with religious ardor. Yet one burst into flames, forcing her jumpers to bail over a densely forested area and her to set down the Twin Otter in a lake barely the size of a pond. She almost died landing, almost died escaping the sinking craft, and almost died avoiding the ensuing inferno. She had spent a sleepless night surrounded by bears, hiked the next morning, only to come upon her father's fallen plane and charred remains, and now . . . to add ridiculous insult to injury, a crazy toothless mountain man was kidnapping her at gunpoint.

Her attempts to spark up conversation were not helpful.

"Do you live back here?"

"Git." Cough and wheeze. "Shut up and git yourself on."

"Why are you pointing that gun at me? I'm not a threat to you. My plane crashed back—"

"You ain't getting it."

Elle had the sense from his inflection that he meant more

than a repeating of his order to stop speaking. "Why would I want to get *it*?"

"Don't play stupid, missy. It's mine. And ain't none of you going to get it."

She could only imagine what he was referring to. The guy was off his nut. Probably a paranoid-schizophrenic. A hoarder. What was *it*? Could be anything that he'd fixed value on. A beaver fur? Some kind of shiny object he found on the ground. She was sure it would have no value to anyone but him.

Whatever it was, he wasn't about to share. So that led to the next question—where was he leading her? Somewhere to die?

She had to keep him talking. She thought of his bloodstained clothing and the pained limp he shuffled along with. "I'm trained in nursing, you know." A blatant lie, but he didn't know that. "I could help you."

The old man kept silent. Maybe he was considering her offer. Elle risked turning her head to see him. His gaze listed to the side, the shotgun barrel tipped toward the ground. His eyes flicked to her and he pointed the gun. "Eyes front."

Her few seconds of recon revealed bad news. Dual hammer. One still cocked. Dad often took her bird hunting in the off-season in Idaho. He usually had her use a pump-action shotgun. Before she could fire, she had to ensure the safety was off, unlock the slide action, chamber a round, and then pull the trigger. Those four steps served as a safeguard. Unfortunately, it appeared that the only thing the old man had to do now was pull the trigger to fire a round.

If she tried to make a move, it could be fatal. The old man was injured—that was clear. He was frail, and she knew she could overpower him if he failed to keep her at gunpoint. Therein lay the rub. His evident psychosis made him a relentless watchdog. How long had he been out here alone, staring nightly into the forest, setting booby traps, and shouting threats into the empty woods? Suddenly he discovered another human fallen from the sky. Surely she was out for his *it*. Whatever it was. She decided to keep on the first-aid idea.

"Why don't you take me to where you live? We can have a look at your wound. I'll clean and dress it for you and . . . and make you a warm meal. Do you have a pot to boil water?"

He wheezed and hacked. Elle tilted her chin down to catch what she could of him in her peripheral vision. All she could make out was the shiny black barrel of the shotgun pointed at her.

He finished his coughing fit. "Haven't had me a woman to cook for some time. Cabin ain't far."

Elle wondered if he ever had a woman to cook for him. Likely not. But if he had, what happened to her? She shuddered at the thoughts that followed.

"This blood here's nothing. I been mauled by a bear worse than this." He coughed again. "I know how to play dead. It's why I'm still living. So don't you get no ideas. I ain't going to let you go and kill me in my sleep. Don't think I don't know what you come for."

CHAPTER 37

Caleb hiked alongside a limping Cleese, who took well to the role of immortal zombie.

Unfeeling, sociopathic. He kept a good pace even with the through-and-through gunshot wound in his foot. After freeing each other from their ties, Caleb doused the wounds with antiseptic, packed dressings on the entrance and exit, and wrapped the foot with gauze from his pack. Cleese acted more perturbed about the hole in his boot leather than anything.

Trudging along, Caleb couldn't tell if his mind fog was more from blurry sleep-deprivation or the effects of the expanding smoke cloud around them. The scent of woodsmoke was pervasive, insidiously invading every fabric and nook. He smelled it when he unzipped his fireline pack, when he took off his helmet, when he unscrewed the lid of his canteen.

Cleese's sheltered eye sockets darkened his expression, lending him an animal-like air. It was like hiking with a wounded wolf, a sinewy sharp-toothed hunter operating on instinct alone.

Caleb understood men like Cleese. No need to befriend him any more than one would a bear or a cougar. If Caleb got bit, or mauled, or killed, it was his own fault. He had to understand the animal, not tame him. By understanding, he was able to enlist him for a purpose.

Cleese appeared strangely at ease. Caleb got the sense Cleese felt freed up after the attacks by Bo and Silas. Their actions unleashed any remaining bonds that might have held him back otherwise. The gloves were off, and the man seemed to relish the fact.

Caleb checked their direction and shifted course to his eleven o'clock. They emerged from the trees and started up a sandy, shale-covered hillside. The sky glowed the colors of rust and sulfur. A fiery thin line snaked across the hillsides less than two miles away.

He picked up his pace, glancing at Cleese to make sure he was keeping up.

His thoughts turned to Silas, a man more similar to himself. As such, he was more difficult. Complex. Principled. Devoted. Unlike Cleese, he and Silas weren't devoid of a moral compass, of an ethical watch. Silas just chose to wind his a bit tighter.

He unscrewed the cap to his water bottle and drank. Even the water tasted like soot. He forced himself to swallow. The smoke cover was good, but it could get too effective. If his Huey pilot couldn't land to escort the cargo, all their efforts, all the violence, would be fruitless. They wouldn't get another chance.

They made the hilltop, and he slid the GPS unit out of his radio chest pouch. He toggled the buttons and watched the murky green graphics shift polygons on the screen. Small concentric circles cycled—their location. Still several miles off, according to the device, a black dot bounced—their destination. Caleb did the math. Three miles an hour for another two hours . . ..

He glanced at his stoic companion. So nice to be beyond earshot of the effusive Sippi and Rapunzel. If all went well, those guys would overtake Silas and the slower, injured Bo Mansfield. They might have the gun, but Sippi and Rapunzel had the advantage of surprise. Of being the hunters. He'd told them to not bother coming back until they knew those two men were dead and had found a way to hide the bodies so no one would find them. With luck, they'd do the deed, and be back in time to help move the booty.

―――――――

Elle smelled the chimney smoke before seeing the cabin. It wafted differently than the pervasive plume of the forest fire. Pungent. Herbal.

To break up her silent march, she once again tried her hand at conversation with her captor. Any information could be useful.

"Are you already cooking something?"

"Maybe."

"I thought you said you wanted a woman to cook you a meal."

"Didn't quite know I was going to find you, now, did I? Seeing as how you're here now, you can serve it to me."

"You going to eat with that shotgun in hand?"

"Got me a pistol too. Don't you try nothing. I'd just as soon shoot you as let you hang around long enough to the point of nagging." He stopped. "There she is."

Elle looked down upon a small, aging log cabin with a low-hanging A-frame roof and three well-trod paths leading up to it.

He motioned with the shotgun. "Take one of those trails."

"What happens if we don't?"

"Bear traps. Already been attacked once. I don't take no chances. Get on now. You'll make a fine hostage for when your gold-hungry friends show up." He forced out a rumbling wheeze. "Them bandits tried to kill me. I know they'll be back. I heard them talking about it when they thought I was dead."

Elle tried to process all the information he'd revealed. He

thought she was in on a plan with some other people to try and . . . steal his gold? Sounded like figments from a disturbed mind. But perhaps his delusions could enable her escape.

"And what do you plan to do to them when they come back? Bribe them? Hold me ransom?"

He smacked his lips and grunted as he worked his way along the trail behind her. She guessed he hadn't really thought the whole thing through.

Her stomach twisted like a wet towel. The thought of hot soup came as a relief. Perhaps it would relax the old man as well, just enough for her to get the upper hand.

He poked her in the back. Elle had to stoop to enter the front door. The old man behind her had no such need. He pointed to a wooden chair in a far corner. The cabin was one room, maybe three hundred square feet at most. She sat and observed as many things about the place as she could, anticipating that he'd soon blindfold her.

A cast-iron stove sat on a brick hearth in the center of the cabin. An active fire within it heated a pot above. Beyond that a small cupboard hung over a wooden counter on the wall. A washbasin lay atop with a pitcher beside it. A narrow single bed with an ancient brass frame sat tucked into a far corner. The man propped the shotgun on his hip, picked up a hot pad, and lifted the pot lid. Elle considered his positioning. It was a small cabin, but she was still a solid five or six steps from him. She crossed her legs and acted as though she were paying little attention to him.

The herbal scent filled the room. Sage, mint. From the corner of her eye she saw him glance her direction before replacing the lid of the pot.

" 'Coon." He pulled up a wooden chair beside a small table

across from the stove. "Caught this one in a trap." He coughed and rested the gun across his lap. He wiped his ashen brow. His eyes were bloodshot.

Elle put on a friendly smile. "Smells wonderful."

"I pick all my own seasonings. Get 'em wild from the woods."

She nodded, acting as interested as if they were on a first date. "How do you know which plants are safe?"

He waved a hand, playing right into it, letting her stroke his ego. "Living out here, you get to know what's good, what's not. You can smell it. Taste it."

"Do you trap all the animals you eat?"

He sniffed. "Just about. Kind of have to." Something of a grin met his cheeks. "Ain't much in the way of ammunition stores out here." He cackled and then hacked in a violent coughing fit. It drew his fist to his face and had him bending over at the side. The gun barrel slid toward the wall.

If he were only a couple steps closer.

Elle rose, pointing to the pot. "Shall I serve you some supper?"

The man gripped the shotgun and trained it on her. The metal shook in his grip, vehemence in his wild eyes. "Git yourself down in that chair, missy."

Elle raised her hands, feigning innocence. "Yes. Of course. I was only trying to—"

"Shut it." The old man stood, walked to a cupboard beyond the stove, and returned with a pair of handcuffs. He tossed them to Elle. "Chain yourself. I don't care how pretty a lady you are. Your friends tried to kill me. They're coming for my gold. And I ain't taking no chances."

Elle caught the handcuffs tossed to her. The old man bared his teeth and trained the shotgun. There was no negotiating this.

The old man pointed and shook the shotgun toward the entrance. "Go. To the door handle. Slide it through."

She moved as deliberate and slow as she could without provoking him. Should she rush at him now? If she shackled herself there was no way she could overcome him. She stopped at the door with her back to the old man and pushed the half-moon bracelets through with their ratcheting sounds.

"You so much as take a step to run and I'll shoot you, woman. I done it before and I'll do it again."

So that's what happened to the last lady. Elle exhaled a quick breath. She stared at the S-shaped iron door handle, cinched the first handcuff around her wrist, and held it up for the man to see. She glanced back. His jaw quivered. His eyes looked angry, nervous, and half glazed.

He shook the gun at her. "Finish it up now."

She kept her eyes on him and ran the handcuff chain between her and the front of the door handle. It gave the sound of passing through the loop. She placed her other hand in front of her and squeezed down the cuff without her wrist inside of it.

"There," Elle said, standing with her body facing the door. "Now, do you want me to stay like this the whole time, or can I at least have a chair to sit in?"

The old man squinted at her for a moment, then relaxed his finger from the trigger and angled the shotgun toward the ceiling. "Ain't you ever learned you no manners, woman? You want something, you better ask for it proper."

Elle would play along. Just move that gun into one hand and come closer. "May I please have a chair to sit in, sir?"

His chest shook and a grin met his mouth. "Now, that's better." He moved the shotgun into one hand, walked over to the dining table, and grabbed another chair by the top rail. He dragged it on two legs across the floor. His demeanor relaxed, and he took on a jocular and cocky tone. "You know, you keep speaking with respect like that, and maybe I'll let you cook us a meal one of these nights."

Elle watched him, waiting. *Closer. Closer. Three more steps.*

One. His grin waned.

Two. Something flicked in his eyes.

Three. Realization set upon him.

Too late.

Elle grabbed the barrel and spun. She cracked her fist hard on his cheekbone, and the shotgun fired.

CHAPTER 38

Caleb set his foot down in a boot print someone had made the night everything had spun out of control. Cleese shadowed him to his right. He lifted his head and focused on the earth-covered entrance they'd been journeying toward.

He licked his lips, eager to claim the stash, his appetite whetted by the endgame. A glance back at Cleese revealed the same set of emotions. Even a wolf grins at the sight of supper.

He cracked his neck and checked his watch. They had to get moving. He started down the small hill. "Let's get as much as we can out to the clearing before—" He bunched up his nose and turned his head. A putrid smell filled his nostrils. "What is that—"

"The bodies. Already decomposing."

Caleb hid his nose in the crook of his elbow. Inside the bunker he lit a wall lantern. Shadows flickered over the bodies in the back corner. They'd piled Pendleton and the old man back there in a hurry. Cleese descended the iron ladder with some difficulty. Caleb followed him into the dank repository, thankful that the stench lessened somewhat. They clicked on their helmet lights and scanned dozens of chests lining the walls. Caleb glanced up the dumbwaiter and reached for the handle on the side of one of the chests. He grunted without moving it. He took a second look at the chest and tried the handle with two hands. The box barely shifted on the dirt floor.

Caleb exhaled and flipped the latch. Cleese opened the top of the chest. Inside lay piles of gold ore. Caleb lifted a palm-sized gold nugget.

Cleese two-handed a larger chunk. "That bird able to handle all this?"

Caleb scanned the room. He'd done the math. "Hueys are made to carry a dozen guys without a problem. We got us four, so that's about eight hundred pounds. That means it should be able to carry around twice our weight in gold with no worries."

A grin curled Cleese's cheek. "How much you think four hundred pounds of gold is worth?"

"About sixteen thousand per pound, brother." Caleb loaded two nuggets on the dumbwaiter. "It ain't all gold, so it needs to be refined before we know how much we actually have, but there'll be plenty for all."

Cleese whistled. "I'm liking this."

"I figured you weren't along just for the fun of it."

"Oh, I'm still hoping I get to stab somebody."

A gunshot fired in the distance.

Cleese cocked his head toward the ceiling. His dark eyes met Caleb's. He hobbled to the ladder and climbed up.

Boots shuffled over the floor above. "Caleb?"

"Yeah?"

"There's only one body up here."

Caleb's gut twisted. He moved to the foot of the ladder. "Pendleton's gone?"

Cleese returned to the top of it and shook his head. "The old man."

Unbelievable. Caleb had seen Cleese shoot him. "Shotgun too?"

He nodded.

Caleb pounded his fist on a ladder rung. "He can't be far. Our Huey's going to be here in less than two hours."

"You keep moving the gold and don't worry about it." Cleese unsheathed his bowie knife and tilted it in the lamplight. "Looks like I'll get to have my cake and eat it too."

———

Silas shivered with the waning adrenaline. His head felt light. The aching gravity of so much loss threatened to anchor him in place. He'd have to grieve Bo later.

He'd grieve Elle forever.

He pushed the thoughts from his mind. He had to channel his anger, focus his grief. His disbelief. His legs moved in the direction that Bo had pointed out for the bunker. He stayed the urge in his muscles to stop, to rest.

What was his plan? He, unarmed, exhausted, against four guys. So many people had died in their quest. Pendleton, a hermit, Monte, Elle, Bo.

For gold—the love of money.

The winds picked up, swaying and rustling the trees. Fire crackled nearby. Silas stripped off his soaked T-shirt and wrung it. The skin across his torso tightened with the breeze. His efforts with the fabric only produced a few drops. He shook it loose and pulled it back over his head.

The forest closed in, thick with choking smoke, heavy with familiar scents. Fire was part of the life and death and cyclical rebirth of the land. It had never been an enemy. Only a force. Something set in motion. As a smokejumper, he corralled it more than extinguished it.

He had never found a home until the first day he wandered

out into the vast granite plateaus and forested peaks and canyons of the Sierra Nevada. A place of peace. Where the bland linear geometry of cities and streets and indifferent people played no role. It existed by the hand of God alone. Independent, wild, and free.

It had beckoned him. Apart from it he'd never known rest. He thought he had found his true love.

Now, as he trudged forward, trying to forget the pain both physical and visceral, the percolating truth he'd been fighting and ignoring set in.

A forest won't love you back.

Trees, boulders, landscape—it all turned an indifferent eye to man. It was no different than the cold drab walls of the San Mateo Home for Boys, no different than the pale concrete streets and repetitive tract homes with family after family carting him around in their four-door sedans, providing a room and collecting a check.

Hot tears welled, surprising him. He just wanted to see Elle— even if it could only be one more time, for only a moment. He needed to tell her that he was wrong, that he had been scared. That he had somehow felt disqualified from having the right to have a family. He didn't have a clue how to have one. His only security and peace had ever come by running and escaping on his own.

With her he'd felt things he'd only dreamed about but never owned the sensation of. The thought of spending his life with her exhilarated and frightened him at the same time.

Ever since that summer when he never showed up for their date, for their sunset picnic, he'd worn an albatross around his neck. He'd known their relationship was at a point of turning.

And the thought of that date, that simple blanket-spread late-summer supper, felt more like *family* than anything Silas had ever known.

Then word came of "Grandma" Jo's illness.

And he bailed. Set off across the mountains, thinking that there he would find himself again, find a sense of stable ground and an understanding of his place in it all.

But he never found a sense of elation or illumination. There wasn't an epiphany or a peace. It was he, scared like a child, running from real love like he'd never known before.

He poured himself into work, into jumping from aircraft and fighting fire. He took every assignment offered and volunteered for more. Jumping didn't fulfill him. It fueled him. It stoked a self-destructive flame inside him. He deserved to be cast toward the earth, among serpents and scorpions, wheat and tares. He garnered experience faster than most his age, and he achieved his promotion, the youngest jumper ever to make it to spotter. What good was it now?

Smoke moved through the trees in long waving banners.

A gunshot echoed.

His attention snapped to a ridge up ahead. He listened. No other shots followed.

Silas ran his hands over his face. Bo was dead. Elle was dead. There was no chance of redemption with her. The most he could do was bring justice to her killers.

He had no means. No plan. No advantage.

And no qualms.

Lord, give me strength.

He steeled his resolve and quickened his pace.

CHAPTER 39

Wood shattered. Elle's hearing deafened. She grabbed the stock of the gun and drove her shoulder against the man's chest. He fought to keep it, circling toward the wall. Elle shoved him against the splintered logs, head-butted him, and pried free the weapon.

She stumbled back, found her balance, and pointed the gun at him. Trembling, he raised his hands. Elle kept her finger pointed straight along the trigger housing, just like Dad taught her. She had no desire to kill anybody. But he didn't have to know that.

"Hands on your head and turn around. Get on your knees."

The man shuffled around and lowered himself with effort to the floor. An empty handcuff dangled from Elle's wrist, swinging like a pendulum.

Her heartbeat drummed. "Where's the key?"

The old man mumbled.

She fought to keep her voice level. "Speak up. Where's the key?"

"I said . . ." He stopped to catch his breath. "In the pantry. Top shelf."

She sidestepped to the kitchen, catching a glimpse of the swelling and contused cheek where she'd struck him. She threw open the pantry doors one-handed. Not tall enough to see the top shelf, she eyed the old man for a moment, then stretched and searched with her fingers. She felt two handcuff keys linked by a beaded chain. Several shotgun cartridges rolled off the shelf.

Elle made quick work of unlocking the wrist bracelet and pocketed the keys. She snagged a shell from the floor, broke open the shotgun action, and replaced the spent round. The old man turned from his kneeling position.

She clicked the weapon closed and aimed. "Eyes front." She slid the handcuffs across the floor beside him. "Role reversal. You know what you need to do."

He glanced sideways at the cuffs.

She wedged the stock against her shoulder. "Door handle. And let me see it go through."

He shifted to his hip, picked up the cuffs, and pushed himself to his feet.

She wished she had a pump-action shotgun. The sound of the slide action communicated volumes. She cocked a hammer.

He stared at her and locked one cuff around a wrist.

"Good." Elle motioned with the barrel. "Now through the handle."

The old man shuffled to the door, threaded the bracelet behind the iron grip, and locked it around his other wrist.

She looked him over, making sure there weren't any tricks he could pull, nothing she'd missed. She directed him with the gun barrel to open the door all the way inward, wide open.

Elle sidestepped toward the exit, never lowering the shotgun, never taking her eyes off of the man. "Back against the wall. Legs forward and toes up."

The old man sneered and leaned back against the wall. He straightened his legs in front of him and rested on his heels.

She paused at the threshold. "I never wanted your gold. If there even is any. My plane crashed, and my jumper crew may have injured members out in the forest." She took a deep breath and shook her head. "Authorities will be back here, if the fire doesn't come this way first. Don't think you've gotten away with anything. You'll be held accountable for your actions."

An insolent grin grew across the old man's bruised face. He cackled. "Lady, it don't matter."

Her eyebrows tightened. This man was disturbed.

He laughed again. "It don't matter. 'Cause I'm going to be dead, and so are you."

A sharp edge pressed against her windpipe. Hot rancid breath met the angle of her jawline. Beneath her chin, an upturned fist with tattooed fingers held a glinting steel blade.

A raspy voice wafted tobacco, "Evening, Pilot. Turns out you're just as hard to kill as our spotter."

CHAPTER 40

Cleese tugged Elle backward from the cabin entrance. Her heart sped. Her breathing shallowed. She lowered the shotgun.

"Nope," he said. "No, no. Keep that barrel pointed up and at our superhuman friend, Mr. Zane Leewood. How you doing in there, old man? I should've double-checked to make sure you were dead. Crazy old fool."

Cleese angled Elle so she could still see the old man through the doorway. "How's that, girly? Can you get 'em from here? Go ahead. Shoot 'em. But make it a good one, 'cause he don't die easy."

Elle felt nauseated. "I . . . I can't do that."

"Nonsense. I do believe this man was holding you prisoner, now, wasn't he? Who knows what kind of plans he had for you. Shoot him."

Elle set the hammer and threw down the shotgun. She couldn't shoot him if she wasn't holding it.

Cleese pulled her head back and pressed the knife to her skin. "That . . . did not make me happy." He exhaled through his nose and angled the point of his knife on her throat.

"Please, I'm a mother." She regretted the words as soon as she said them.

Cleese feigned a gasp. "My, my. A *mother.*" He twisted the blade back and forth and began to sing, "My mother and your mother right were hanging up clothes. My mother punched your mother right in the nose. What color was. Her. Blood." He pierced her skin.

Elle stifled a cry as the burning sting heightened. A hot trickle rolled down her neck, pooling in the upper angle of her sternum.

"Old man," Cleese said, "you're just going to have to wait to be finished off. You hear? Me and the pilot have some business to attend to." He forced her backward, taking one step at a time.

She squeezed tight her eyes. *God, help me. God, help me.* She opened them and saw Zane crouched by the door handle in the semi-darkness of his cabin, eyes darting between her and Cleese and the path he walked her back on.

The paths.

Elle scanned the ground around them. All the old man's well-worn tracks followed three different routes, none of which they were walking on now.

She swallowed, taking metered steps with Cleese. He was saying something, lilting and monologuing, appearing perfectly at ease with the situation at hand.

He took a limping step back. And another. Before the very next Elle looked back at the old man. His eyes grew wide.

The bear trap sprang.

Cleese shouted and loosened his grip. Elle grabbed his knife-wielding arm with both hands and pushed it away from her neck. She dove away and rolled to her feet.

He let out an agonized cry, shock in his face. His right leg bent at an obtuse angle just below the knee, where the jaws of the bear trap came together. Out of his reach but not on one of the old man's paths, Elle froze, realizing she could be inches away from the same fate as Cleese. Cleese writhed and cursed, the knife still in his grip. Just behind her, Elle spotted the path. She took one long step onto it and backed away.

Just run.

But she couldn't take her eyes off of him. The second she turned he might hurl the blade at her back.

Get out of here.

Cleese still paid her no attention. The path she backed along led right to the cabin. From there she could get on the path she'd arrived on with the old man and run up the hill, away from all this. She quickened her backward pace. Just a few more steps to the cabin.

Something clicked in Cleese's face. The shock had worn off. In one instant he shut out the pain, in the next he fixed his fury on Elle. He pinched the knife blade between his thumb and forefinger and held it up by his head.

Elle stumbled backward and collided with the cabin. Stunned, she shot a glance up the hill path. She was only about twelve feet away—still within throwing distance.

Cleese bared his spaced-tooth grin. "Looks like you ain't going to get out of this after all." His arm cocked. His eyes widened. Elle scrambled for the cabin door.

A gunshot blasted.

Cleese collapsed forward, falling face down on the dirt. A blood pool floated the dust around him.

Electrical tension coursed through Elle's body. Staccato breaths. Beading sweat. Standing in the doorway, one handcuff hanging free from his wrist, the old man held the shotgun at his shoulder, the barrel still pointed toward Cleese, who lay in the dirt.

Zane cracked his neck and lowered the weapon. "Been

wanting to do that." He turned toward Elle. "Come on now, woman. Did you really think I wouldn't keep an extra set of keys on my person?"

His chest shook with a building coughing fit. He pushed his lips together to try and hold it in, which only made him convulse more violently. The coughing finally escaped with potent hacking. He spat and brought the gun to bear on Elle.

"Now, little lady, this here fellow obviously had no love for you. But that don't mean I believe you none. You could just as easily be one of another party out to get to my stash. I ain't no fool. I done survived out here for years, and now you see why." He sniffed and ran his tongue along his bottom lip. "So I suppose we're just about back to where we started now, ain't we."

CHAPTER 41

Another gunshot. Sweat dripped from Caleb's brow and soaked into the rugged wood beneath him. He straightened and massaged his lower back, glancing again at the path to the prospector's cabin.

What's going on, Cleese?

Caleb was torn. Not out of particular loyalty to Cleese. But because he knew that keeping him happy was key to getting his own share out of all this. That, and Caleb was making pitifully slow progress on moving the gold into the clearing. He'd had to first empty half of each chest in the basement of the storage cache in order to even be able to scoot the chest onto and off of the dumbwaiter and then outside from there.

He was beginning to worry. Cleese was a capable and ruthless man. But Caleb had already seen Cleese bested once by Silas. If Silas and Bo were still out there and managed to get the upper hand on Sippi and Rapunzel, who were chasing them without a weapon . . .

Caleb exhaled, realizing the idiocy of his plan as he reconsidered its merits. Was it destined to fail? What had he been thinking? In his lust for the gold, had he already made mistakes that doomed his mission to failure?

"No." Caleb shook his head and whispered, "No. This is ours. Ours by right."

The beating of helicopter blades sounded in the distance. Caleb squinted into the diffuse smoky light overhead. His pilot was going to have to come in on instruments and instinct. Caleb switched his radio to a local line-of-sight channel. No repeater necessary or desired. Radio waves could carry a bit without a repeater, but given their remote position, no one should overhear them. Once the chopper cleared the haze overhead, he should have enough visibility to touch down.

Caleb chewed the inside of his cheek. It was going to be close.

He depressed the transmit button on his Handie-Talkie. "Bluebird, this is Ground. How do you copy?"

The radio squelched and sat silent in Caleb's chest pack. He tried again with the same transmission.

The sound of the helicopter grew louder. Caleb took a deep breath and resolved to move another load of the gold. Once he got that up, he'd attempt to contact the Huey again.

If only Cleese would get back soon, he'd have some help. He descended the ladder and loaded up another half-filled chest onto the dumbwaiter. He hoisted the load to the first level, his gloves wearing thin from the work, and dragged the chest one side at a time onto the floor.

His radio squawked. "Ground, this is Bluebird. I'm over your location but don't have eyes on you."

Caleb dropped the end of the chest in the opening of the bunker. He caught his breath and replied, "Copy, Bluebird. Stand by."

He pulled his GPS from his pocket and walked to the place he'd marked for the landing zone. The last digits flipped into place, and he radioed the exact coordinates to the chopper. "Descend at those coordinates and you should have eyes on the LZ at about two hundred feet."

"Copy that, Ground."

Caleb pulled four fusees from his pack and struck their sulfur heads. Pink flames shot from the ends as he dropped one at each of the four corners of the fifty-foot-by-fifty-foot landing zone. Not a ton of room, but enough for Jake to set her down safely.

The heavy helicopter blades hacked through the air overhead. The smoke cloud hanging overhead swirled and shook. Two landing skids emerged, followed by the white steel body of the chopper.

"Bluebird, I've got eyes on you now. Maintain your trajectory."

"Copy that, Ground. I've got a visual on the LZ."

The Huey lowered, and the noise intensified. Pebbles and dirt went airborne. Caleb shielded his face and found refuge in the opening to the cache.

Jake angled the tail rotor away from the cache and toward one of the far fusee. He tapped one landing skid down and then the next. The helicopter rested into position, and the engines cut off with a decrescendoing whine.

The rotor blades spun down and the pilot's door opened. Jake climbed down and walked over. He shook hands with Caleb. "So what? Nobody show up to your party?"

Caleb wasn't exactly in a jovial mood. "Things haven't gone as planned."

Jake cocked his head.

A voice shouted from the small hill beyond the cache. "Caleb."

Sippi descended. Rapunzel lumbered after him.

Sippi eyed Jake and held Caleb's pistol in the air. "Mansfield's dead."

Caleb spat. So much for keeping Jake in the dark. "You're sure?"

"Shot him myself. The body floated to shore."

Jake pocketed his hands and glanced at the helicopter.

Caleb drew a breath. "What about the spotter?"

Rapunzel limped over. "He's in the lake—shot or drowned."

Caleb looked from Rapunzel to Sippi. "That right, Sippi? You know he's dead?"

Sippi sniffed. "I shot several rounds at both those guys. Bo floated to the edge. Kent's body drifted to the middle of the lake."

The skin at Caleb's temples tightened. "Crystal Lake?"

He nodded.

"You see the plane?"

"No sign of it. Busted-up treetop. That's it."

"What'd you do with Bo's body?"

Rapunzel scratched his beard. "We left him on the shore."

"And you couldn't see your way to retrieving Kent's body?"

Sippi jutted his chin. "He was way out there, Caleb. Was already sinking by the time we got done checking Bo."

Caleb turned and put his hands behind his head. "All right. We'll figure it out. No one but us knows the pilot aimed to put the plane down there. For now just forget it. Good enough. Now give me the gun."

Sippi studied him.

"Give it to me."

Sippi turned the grip toward Caleb and flashed a glance at Rapunzel. "Only one round left."

Caleb snatched the weapon, checked the safety, and tucked it in his belt. "You get the other clip?"

"I didn't know they had—"

"Never mind." Caleb exhaled. "This is Jake. He's our ticket out of here. The man doesn't work for free. He gets an equal cut. With Monte and Bo gone, that means more for the rest of us. Help him get all this loaded up."

Rapunzel huffed. "Where you going?"

"To find Cleese. There's been gunshots."

"Thought that's what we heard."

"The old man's body is gone. So he went to try to find him."

"Oh? And you just figured you'd leave out that little detail."

"We're on a time schedule. With these winds, the fire'll be upon us anytime. I'll just make a quick search. Jake, if we're not back in twenty minutes, take off without us. We'll rendezvous at the secondary landing zone at the time we arranged. You've got the coordinates, right?"

The pilot nodded.

Caleb eyed the men. Fatigue shadowed their faces. Their enthusiasm waned. Caleb knew the cure. He walked to one of the storage chests and kicked the top open. Gold nuggets glinted. Eyes widened.

"That, fellas, is the payoff. We're almost there. As far as anyone knows, we all perished with Jumper 41. Load up this booty and we can, each of us, inherit life anew."

CHAPTER 42

Elle leaned her head against the wooden door. Her hands hung cuffed, this time to the inside handle with the door shut. She sat with her legs bent together. The old man wheezed and coughed and searched for something in the kitchen pantry. His hands trembled and clumsily knocked over spice jars. The shotgun stood propped in the corner.

Cleese's body lay out front.

The old man staggered, mumbling to himself. His skin color became ashen. He rummaged about, as though he were at work to prepare a meal, but his efforts accomplished little to nothing. A pot on the cast-iron stove boiled over, water hissing and vaporizing on contact with the surface.

He fell victim to a hacking and coughing fit, balancing on the counter for support. The coughing continued, and then, in one violent sudden cessation, he stood erect, clutched his chest, and looked at Elle with eyes like a man falling into an abyss.

———————

Caleb squinted through the growing smoke. The sound of the fire crackled constantly now. The front was hitting even sooner than he expected.

He held his Ruger in his hand, ring finger threaded through the top of the trigger well, handgrip pointed downward. Last thing he needed was to shoot himself in the leg. He strode along the trail, eyes beginning to water from the smoke. He stopped at the tree line before the cabin and blinked away the moisture. The door was shut and the wick of an oil lantern emitted a warm glow through a small window.

His eyes fell to a form facedown in the dirt. Caleb drew a sharp breath.

Cleese. His knife lay beside him in the dust. One of his legs bent at an unnatural angle, clamped between the jaws of a saw-toothed bear trap.

Caleb clicked off the pistol safety and chambered a round. Maybe this was foolhardy. The prudent choice would be to cut his losses and bail, but he couldn't leave any witnesses.

He angled the Ruger in front of him and studied the perimeter. Three well-trod paths led to the front door of the cabin. From the looks of Cleese's fate, Caleb thought it wise to stick to those. He walked sideways down the path toward the front door. His eyes bounced from corner to corner of the cabin and then back to the window. He made out a kitchen counter and a hanging pantry with cabinet doors ajar.

How best to do this?

Caleb reached the front door and turned his back against the wall, peering through the window for evidence of anyone inside. On the floor just beyond the table, barely distinguishable in the faint lantern light, lay a dark object—possibly a body?

The front door rattled.

Caleb jumped back and swallowed a curse. He pressed against the cabin wall and aimed his gun at the door.

———

Silas felt light-headed and short of breath. The smoke-veiled edges of the forest lit aglow. A pervasive pop and crackle filled the air.

From somewhere close came a distinct mechanical sound. He placed hands on his knees and inclined his ear. Rotors. A Bell UH-1. Since his time years ago on a helitack crew, he couldn't mistake it. A Huey was taking off, from somewhere very close.

The temperature elevated. He ran, advancing with the flame front. Ash flittered in the breeze. Fire fingered alongside, jumping and spotting flames up ahead.

A blast of thick dark smoke chugged from a juniper ahead of him.

Branches cracked beneath his heels. Rocks tumbled beneath his boots. One more hillside. One more obstacle to surmount.

He crested the hill in time to see the skids of a helicopter lifting into the smoke above.

Silas dropped to his knees. Oxygen fled from his lungs. He blinked and gasped, propping himself with one hand.

Cunning plan. Sabotage the jumper aircraft. Drop into an area under conditions they knew no one would chase them into. Grab the hidden plunder and coordinate a rendezvous with a getaway bird. The Huey had the carrying capacity to fly out all of those guys and a heavy load of gold.

The wind swirled soot and dust. The fire would soon be upon him.

———

The door shook again. A voice grunted. Caleb's hamstrings ached and his forearms tired.

Metal clacked and wood knocked again, followed by an exasperated sigh. A sigh . . . not a grunt. A woman's sigh.

Caleb stood alongside the window. He stuck his head out with more boldness to examine the shape on the floor of the kitchen. Sure enough, those were boots, and the boots were attached to the legs and torso of the old prospector on his back. Unless he had decided to take an impromptu nap, Caleb guessed he was out of commission. He moved more in front of the window and turned his gaze to the opposite side of the front door. There, of all people, sat the pilot, handcuffed to the handle.

His eyes flicked back to Cleese and the dark muddy blood pool beneath him.

A breathy laugh escaped. He shook his head.

Impressive. And irritating.

He scanned the edges of the small clearing around the cabin. An orange glow filled the forest, smoke lingering in the spaces like an army of specters.

Caleb really preferred not to be on the front end of killing. Okay, murder. Call it what it was. That's where Cleese had proved useful. The man had no reluctance of conscience or squeamishness of gut.

Caleb saw the greater plan as it needed to be. And he'd designed the operation so there would be no face-to-face killings.

When Plan A didn't work, he had hoped to fall back on Cleese to carry out the details by the more grotesque means. But even that, as most things on their mission, had failed. The spotter and Bo escaped, prompting him to send off two more men, away from the gold, for the purpose of finishing what could have been so cleanly accomplished by an apparent aviation accident.

Enough remorse. Fate found him now with the upper hand and the fortune in flight. The fire would soon be upon this place and take it to the ground. He placed his hand on the wrought-iron door handle and depressed the latch.

———————

Silas lifted his head at the sight of motion along the clearing's edge.

Caleb burst from a narrow forest path with another person. *Elle.*

Alive.

She staggered behind him, her hair balled in his fist, hands cuffed behind her back.

Smoke flooded the area. The pressing flames advanced with a dull roar. Below, Caleb dragged Elle across the clearing to an earthen mound that, on closer inspection, sported a rectangular opening reinforced by timbers.

The bunker.

They disappeared inside of it. Silas hopped to his feet. He ran and jumped along the edge until he reached the top of the earth-covered bunker. He lowered to a squat and crawled forward, floating ash fluttered past his head. He felt the heat of the fire on the backs of his legs. The clearing beneath him reeled into view with every movement forward until he came to just above the edge.

Voices trailed out. Elle's, sorrowful and burdened. "This is insane. You understand that? Look at me. Look at me and tell me what you are doing."

"The time is past for explanations, Pilot." Caleb's voice, accompanied by the sound of scuffling and something like a reel unwinding.

"My name is Elle. You know it. Look at me. Look at me and face what you are doing."

"What I am doing, *Elle,* is what needs to be done. I cannot take any chances with you this time."

"What you're doing is murder."

"Call it what you will."

"There's no other name for it."

"I've spent my life corralling fate, Elle. You know that? As a medic, I curbed death until it found another way in through the cracks. And now, as a smokejumper, what do I do? What do we do? We herd fire in the direction we want it to go. Sometimes you need to give fate some direction. I am sorry it had to work out this way." The scuffling grew louder. Caleb paused in the entryway, a wooden dowel in hand with cord spooling out from it. "It will be swift. You won't suffer."

Silas's eyes grew wide. A cord fuse. Caleb was going to blow the bunker and bury Elle with it.

Erratic winds howled. Fire lapped into the perimeter trees, flaring them off like Roman candles.

Caleb moved backward, both hands on the cord reel. Both hands meant neither held a gun.

Silas perched on the balls of his feet. Flaming embers flitted. He counted down.

Three. Hands at the ready.

Two. Foot on the threshold.

One.

CHAPTER 43

Elle screamed. Caleb dropped to the dirt, jumped by another man. The two tangled and twisted.

Silas.

Unbelief and excitement filled her. She jerked her handcuffs against the pipe railing beside the pulley system. The bolts in the aging boards below jiggled. She grabbed the metal crossbar with both hands and shook, trying to increase the play in the railing, rattling the handle of a push broom that leaned against the far end of it. On instinct, she slid the cuffs along the pipe and reached toward the bolts below. The metal bracelets dug into her wrist.

Silas and Caleb exchanged blows. Silas struck Caleb twice in the face. Caleb swung a fist to his belly. The two locked like steers again. Caleb pulled the gun from his belt, but Silas grabbed his wrist and took him to the ground. The gun fired. Silas knocked Caleb's wrist against a stone. The pistol went flying, and the two tumbled in the duff. Sagebrush in the clearing burst into flame. Cheatgrass at their boots ignited. Smoke curled inside the bunker.

Elle rattled and fought against the metal. Her hair draped over her face. She flipped it back, strands sticking to the sweat across her brow. The men rolled over blackened and smoking ground, flames licking up around them. Elle's eyes followed a line of grass catching fire. It wound directly beneath the fuse reel.

The fire roared in the wind. "Silas!"

He wrapped his arm over Caleb's back and glanced over at her, cheeks red and hair wild.

"The fuse." She pointed. "The fire is going for the fuse."

Caleb grunted and lifted Silas at the midsection. He drove him up and then back down into the earth. Flames flashed across the cheatgrass, wicking toward the fuse. Silas shifted to his knees. He drove an elbow into Caleb and clambered to his feet.

The fire licked at the fuse. Silas lunged for the cord, lifted it from the ground and shot a glance back at Elle.

Caleb barreled into Silas, knocking him to the ground and the cord from his grasp. The fuse fell into the burning grass. Silas made his belly and struggled for the fuse. But Caleb pounded fists against his ears and jaw.

Silas covered his head, kicked and turned and ended up on his back. Caleb shifted and positioned himself on Silas's chest, taking full advantage to drive fist blows to his face. Silas writhed and struggled but was pinned beneath the punishment.

Helpless, Elle watched blow after blow strike him. His arms dropped lower, his strength to block the barrage waning, opening his head to even more strikes.

"Silas!"

He didn't look her way.

Hot, stinging tears welled in her eyes. Elle shook the railing, screaming in frustration.

"Stop it. Stop it!"

Caleb gripped Silas's shirt with one fist and landed another blow with his opposite. Silas's head dropped to the side. His eyes rolled back. Caleb cocked his fist above his head.

The fuse lit.

It hissed and sparkled and took off in two directions—one

up into the cord reel, where it quickly burned out. The other climbed along the cord that ran straight toward the middle of the bunker a body length from Elle and toward several stacks of dynamite Caleb had moved from the walls.

Caleb released Silas and stood. He stared at the fuse and flashed a wild, panicked look at Elle. He turned, stumbled, scampered to his feet, and ran off into the forest beyond.

The fire buzzed along the fuse. She had half a minute at most. Elle shook the railing again. Silas lay unconscious.

There had to be a way.

Sparks ran along the fuse, drawing closer. The world around Silas lay engulfed in wind-driven smoke.

Seconds remained.

It wasn't supposed to end like this.

She brought her hand to her mouth and let it fall to her chest. She felt the circle of her father's ring hanging on her necklace.

The necklace.

Her eyes flashed to the push broom just out of reach. She lowered her head and pulled off the chain. The lit fuse climbed toward the entrance. She hooked a finger through the ring, brought her hands above the railing, and flipped the necklace toward the top of the broom handle.

It knocked against the wood and swung back. The fuse sparked inside the bunker, running up the middle of the floor toward the explosive stash.

Elle held the necklace up and flipped it again. The chain sailed over the end of the handle and slid down the shaft. She yanked the broom toward her. It tipped like a tree into her hands.

Elle shifted her feet around, lifted the end of the broom handle and spun the flat wood atop the brushes toward the ground. The fire danced along the cord, hissing and spitting. She hovered the broom head over the fuse cord, her forearms burning, sweat beading. Waiting. Waiting, until the sparking inched just within her reach.

She slammed the broom end upon it. Again and again, the cuffs biting into her skin. She pummeled the fuse, driving up dirt and pebbles. Wood cracked with a swing and the brush head broke off and flipped across the floor.

She trembled with the shattered broom handle in hand. Dust fell to the floor. And there the fuse lay darkened and burnt up to the point where she struck it.

No more sparking. No more hissing.

She collapsed by the pipe railing, chest heaving for breath. She ran fingers over gashes in her wrists, over the skin of her palms now worn raw. The necklace chain draped across her knuckles, running through her father's ring upon her finger.

CHAPTER 44

The sound of rotors beating in the air brought Elle's head up. Silas stirred outside. A storm of ash and dirt swirled about him. A helicopter descended. Black-clad gunmen deployed across the darkened patches of cheatgrass. One came to Silas's side while others charged into the bunker.

Shouting. Voices. A man knelt by her and unlocked her cuffs. His face looked caring and confident. The name *Anderson* lay stitched in white lettering against a rectangular black patch on his vest. The backs of others read *FBI* in large lettering.

"We're glad to see you alive, Captain Westmore."

Elle blinked, fighting the haze in her vision and the pervasive exhaustion throughout her body. "How?"

"You tell me, ma'am."

She licked her chapped lips. "No, I . . . How did you find us?"

"We had a tip-off about the heist and were en route here to apprehend additional suspects."

"Additional?"

"Yes. We took two men into custody when they landed with their stolen cargo, and another at a separate rendezvous point."

"Is Silas . . ."

"He's battered but awake. We have a medic with him now."

Outside, several men lifted Silas onto a cot. Elle touched her cheek. She took a deep breath and turned to Anderson. "You're still looking for Cleese."

"Yes." He pulled a notepad from his vest pocket. "And men by the names of Monte and Mansfield."

"Cleese is dead."

"Do you know where the body is?"

"About a quarter mile from here. Shot by an old man who lived in a cabin. That man is dead as well."

He nodded and scribbled on his notepad. "What about the other two?"

Elle shook her head. "I don't know."

"That's all right."

"Who tipped you guys off?"

"Mr. Parson's helicopter pilot was of great help to us. He'd been approached by Parson about flying out an undisclosed cargo for an appreciable sum. No questions. All covert. When the pilot learned your aircraft had gone down, he grew suspicious. Said he'd already taken part in a search for one Westmore a couple years back."

"My father."

"I'm sorry for your loss."

"It's okay."

"The pilot needed the money, but he wasn't willing to be a party to murder. That's when he contacted us."

Two men girded in olive green Kevlar walked into the bunker. They examined the extinguished fuse and the dynamite stash.

One shook his head. "Lucky it didn't get hotter in here." He faced Anderson. "Lieutenant, we need to clear everyone from this area as soon as possible."

"C'mon." Anderson extended his hand. "Let's get you to safety and medical attention."

She stood with his assistance.

He led her outside. "We'll fly you back."

Four men strode toward the helicopter with Silas on the cot. They slid him inside on the floor. A medic and an agent climbed in.

Anderson guided Elle up to a seat in the helicopter, pointed to the five-point seat belt harness, and handed her a helmet.

She tucked her hair back and slid it on. "Thank you."

Anderson nodded and slid the door shut.

Lying on the floor in front of her, Silas twitched his eyes and opened them. His muscles tensed, and he tried to sit up. "The fuse—"

She stretched out and patted his arm. "It's okay. It's okay. We're safe."

He looked at her hands. His voice came out raspy, "Caleb?"

"They caught him. The FBI caught him. The others too."

She saw the confusion in his soot-streaked and bloodied face, in his red-tinged eyes ringed with purple bruising. He searched her for answers. "I don't understand."

Elle smiled and shook her head. "Neither do I." She squeezed his fingers.

He winced.

"Oh." She relaxed her grip, noticing the redness with scattered small blisters across his skin. "You're burned."

The medic put a hand on Silas's shoulder. "Sir, you should lie back."

"I'm all right. It's all right." Silas propped himself up and looked at his arms. "It's not too bad." He coughed. "Just a sunburn."

The medic moistened dressings with sterile saline and wrapped them around Silas's burns.

"Thanks." Silas held up a wrapped hand. "That's good. Really." He fought back another cough. "Thank you."

The medic eyed him, glanced at Elle, and then relented and returned to his seat.

Silas's eyes fell to the ring on her forefinger, the chain still curled in her palm.

His mouth seemed to search for words. "I thought—I thought you were . . ."

She shook her head.

His eyebrows angled. "What is it?"

"I found him." She swallowed. She let the ring dangle on the necklace. "My father."

He took the ring in hand. He touched his brow with his other and flinched at the contact with the bruised skin. He shook his head. "I have so many questions."

Moisture brimmed in her eyes. "Me too."

He brought his unwrapped hand to hers. "I didn't mean to jump out of the plane."

Elle broke out in a smile. She laughed. "I know. I know you didn't."

"I didn't want to leave." He coughed again—this time gripping his side. "I didn't want to leave you. Not again. I never should have."

Elle shook her head. "You don't have to—"

"No. I do." He looked around the helicopter, at the stone-faced men in place beside them. "How did we . . . ? I don't know how any of this . . . how Caleb . . . the fuse . . . ?" His eyes returned to her. "My head really hurts."

She pushed her lips together. A tear flipped off her chin. "Here, lie down. You should lie down."

"No, I'm good."

"You're not good. You're stubborn."

"Elle."

"Yeah?"

"I came for you. From the second I hit the ground, I was coming for you."

"I know."

"Being ripped away . . . I thought you were dead."

A hand pounded the door twice. Men outside strode away from the helicopter.

He swallowed, eyes focused on her from behind puffy, purple skin. "I know now. I realized."

The engines whined into high idle.

He interlaced his fingers with hers. "I've never known a home until now."

Her insides braided like rope. The rotors chopped through the air. Dust and ash scurried in a rising cloud. The helicopter lifted. They rose above the tree line, through the smoky ceiling, and burst into the open air.

He caressed her ring finger. "Elle?"

He held up her father's ring.

"Silas? What are—"

"Wait." He grimaced and took a knee in front of her.

"Silas, no. You—"

His Adam's apple shifted. "Be my wife."

She shook her head. "You've taken too many blows to your head."

He filled his chest with air and straightened. The medic and agent looked on with curiosity.

She felt fingers at her chin. He brought it to face him.

She angled her eyebrows. "Silas. You're battered and dirty and . . ." She shook her head. And . . . *irresistible.* She put a hand on his chest. "You need rest."

He shook his head and leaned forward.

She drew a breath.

His scratchy chin bristled by her cheek. She closed her eyes, heart fluttering. His lips met hers in a gentle kiss.

He pulled back, his familiar surfer-boy grin beneath swollen lips. "I know I look like I just got beat up. I do. I did. I did just get beat up. I know I can be obstinate and arrogant and—Elle, *this* . . . having you, is something that I knew I wanted before that engine exploded. Before I thought I would never have the chance to tell you."

He lifted her father's ring and slid it on her finger. "Forgive me. If you somehow can for leaving you, then I promise to be yours and to make my home with you and with Maddie."

Elle covered her mouth. A salty stream met the corner of her lips. She exhaled, smiled, and wiped the tears from her eyes. "Silas . . ." She slid the ring off of her finger. "Silas, everything has been moving really fast lately."

"I know what I want."

"It—"

"You have to believe me."

"It's not that I don't want you." She glanced at the men, who shifted their gazes. She squeezed the ring. "I've made the mistake of moving too fast before."

He looked away.

She found his eyes. "I want to build this the right way, this time."

He brought a hand over her fist and nodded. "Then I can

wait." His eyes locked with hers. "As long as it takes. I'll wait for you."

Warmth spread within her. She clicked off her seat belt harness and leaned close to him. She threaded fingers through his tousled hair, took his bruised cheeks in her hands, and kissed him.

"I believe you."

CHAPTER 45

At the nurses' counter, Silas signed the last form needed to check out of the Barton Memorial ER in South Lake Tahoe. Madison sat on Elle's lap in a chair along the wall, unable to escape her mother's embrace since they returned. The girl kept looking up at him with starry-eyed awe. She didn't seem to mind his bruises. Elle had told her he earned them while fighting for her.

Elle smiled at her daughter, looked at Silas, and gently bit her lip. "How are you?"

"Bruised not beaten. I see Madison is in good health. Any new leads?"

She brightened. "Yes, actually."

"From a neurologist at this hospital?"

"That's the amazing thing. It didn't come from a doctor. An EEG tech caught an abnormality that had escaped everyone else."

"That's incredible. How?"

"Well, he's been looking at electroencephalograms for years. He has a lot of experience. He told me that when Maddie's images came on the screen, he didn't see anything and was going to save the file and move on to the next case, but he felt prompted to study it again. That's when he saw an abnormality along the central sulcus of the brain."

"What part is that?"

"It's a fissure down the middle of the brain. Something didn't look right about it, so he forwarded his concern to the resident neurologist here. Turns out he had localized the cause of the seizures. The neurologist said it's called Benign Rolandic Epilepsy. Knowing the cause enabled him to prescribe some specific things that should dramatically limit future seizures. But the best part is, by the time she's thirteen or so, she'll have outgrown the condition altogether. It's completely temporary."

Silas shook his head and grinned. "Sounds like an answer to your prayers."

"It really is."

Weathers strode down the corridor with his wife.

"Chief."

He presented a hand to Silas. "Thanks for bringing home our best pilot, son."

The shake pained his sore knuckles. He turned a wince into a smile. "I'm afraid that story is backward, Chief. It's Captain Westmore here who saved me."

He winked at her. "Can't say I'm surprised with that one. How's little Madison doing?"

Elle glanced from Silas to Maddie and stroked her little girl's arms. "Very, very good."

————

Silas cut into the steak Mrs. Weathers grilled for them back at their Tahoe cabin. A couple days had given him the ability to chew without too much pain. With Chief Shivner arrested after Silas related to the FBI incriminating info given to him by Bo, the Feds wanted fresh management put in place and the opportunity to question all those in the original Command staff. Weathers seemed uncomfortable with the time off and no longer being in the fray.

He stared at his plate. "I spoke with Mansfield's sisters the other day. Breaking the news was difficult, to say the least."

Silas nodded. "We owe him our lives."

Madison fidgeted in her seat and squished the mashed potatoes with her fork. Elle set a hand atop Maddie's and admonished her to eat and not play.

Weathers straightened. "I've scheduled a line-of-duty-death memorial for him to be held in two weeks. It will coincide with Pendleton's."

"What about Monte?"

"Given the sketchy details surrounding Pendleton's death, a quiet family service is being held instead. Everything so far points to him being part of the plan to kill the both of you." His brows furrowed. "Too often Forest Service memorials are for multiple firemen. I'd hoped I had attended my last."

Silas stared at the bending colors in his water glass.

Weathers stabbed a bite with his fork. "On another note, I received a call today about the gold find."

Elle replaced Maddie's napkin across her legs. "What did you learn?"

He glanced at Maddie, who was absorbed in a song she sang quietly as she pushed food around on her plate. "The flame front consumed not only the cabin but most of the old man's remains. But the FBI ran a search on a few personal record fragments and discovered a relative back east. A distant cousin.

"Come to find out, this relative knew about the gold but not the man. According to him, the gold cache was something of a family legend. He wasn't aware of its exact location and had never been interested in finding it."

Silas swallowed. "Millions of dollars of gold, and he wasn't interested in finding it?"

"To be fair, the man is well-off." He took a bite.

"But . . ."

"But, you're right—that's not the real reason. According to the FBI, two of the man's ancestors, brothers, lived out west in the 1800s. They staked claim to a large gold find on the 4th of July."

"The Independence Find."

"As you know, a number of miners were injured and some killed under the brothers' watch, and the workers' families received nothing. After a fatal collapse involving one of the brothers and the surviving brother's wife, the surviving brother shut down the mine and took the next several months packing out the ore by mule deep into the wilderness, where we now know he stored it inside a secret underground vault."

Elle nodded. "The bunker we came across."

"Nobody knows for sure why he hid it. Thought it was cursed? Maybe the guilt associated with it was too much. The sole knowledge of its location almost passed with him on his deathbed. He spent the last years of his life tortured by a growing mental illness and in the midst of a paranoid delusion, he divulged his secret to a family member. It took on the form of a familial legend and was passed on as such through the generations."

"The sins of the father . . ."

"To the family, if the legend was true, it was blood money. They chose to keep it a buried secret. Perhaps a penance of sorts."

Silas set down his steak knife. "Not to mention a protection from lawsuits."

Elle shifted in her seat. "From the surviving families of the miners who died. But how did the man from the cabin find it?"

"I asked the same thing. Apparently, deeper into the interview, the wealthy man mentioned a story his father told him about a cousin who also suffered from mental illness. The cousin had shown up one evening at their home asking for money. He spoke of setting out on a backpacking trip in the west. The father sent him off with a hundred dollars, and the cousin was never heard from again."

Silas scratched the back of his neck. "So he discovered the gold cache and wanted to keep it for himself?"

Weathers shrugged. "That, or he felt compelled for some reason to be its guardian. I'm not a psychiatrist, but the FBI profile inferred that the old man's motives might have been driven by transference of his own guilt for something onto the crimes associated with the gold. I don't know. It's over my head."

Elle huffed. "And Shivner thought he could just sail off into the sunset with the gold then, didn't he?"

Weathers raised and lowered his eyebrows. "Didn't count on the gold having a guardian. Since it legally belongs to the surviving family, the Feds needed to know what their wishes were. Ninety percent will be set aside for descendents of the miners injured or killed in the family's gold operation. Of the remaining ten percent, they requested five go to Bo Mansfield's next of kin and the other five to Pendleton's."

Silas breathed deep. "Bo asked me to see to his sisters. To make sure they were okay."

"This will provide more than enough to pay for their educations and to buy homes, if that's what they'd like." Weathers lifted his glass. "To the lost, then." He glanced from Silas to Elle. "And to the found."

CHAPTER 46

Again at the doorway, one foot from the slipstream.

Silas cinched the parachute straps over Elle's white lace dress, shaking his head with the thought of how fast the past year flipped by.

Wind whipped through her curled locks. A pair of goggles rested on her forehead, and a new diamond band shined on her finger. Silas pulled her against his pressed black tuxedo and tightened everything down for their tandem jump. He ran his thumb along the unfamiliar band on his own ring finger. An unending circle, once worn by her father.

The engines roared. Verdant hillsides rolled out below them. Madison sat on the bench seat, strapped between the Weatherses. She grinned, gripping Rose tight in her lap.

Elle set her goggles in place and blew her a kiss. Silas waved. Elle leaned back. "You sure you're ready for this, Kent?"

He wrapped his arms around her waist and shouted over the din. "I can't help but follow you."

She laced her fingers with his.

Three.

Hands on the doorframe.

Two.

Feet on the threshold.

One.

ACKNOWLEDGMENTS

Thank you to all who stood with me through this long-fought and rewarding labor.

To Jesus—there is no greater joy than walking in step with you.

To Sarah Beth, my constant companion and beloved bride—thank you for your unwavering support and partnership throughout.

To my children—Daniel, Claire, and Noah—you are our wonderful joy.

To my mom—somehow you made it into this book as well. No surprise there. Thank you for the gift of your abundant love.

To our treasured parents and all our extended family—for your continued support and advocacy.

Thank you to Karen Schurrer for her intuitive editing, to Dave Long for his support for this story, to Noelle Buss for all the publicity support, and to the entire talented team at Bethany House Publishers.

Thanks to Janet Grant for your wise counsel and savvy representation.

To Mike Berrier, Katie Cushman, Carrie Padgett, and all those who've been there since the beginning—you're my brothers and sisters of the pen.

Special thanks to former smokejumper Pete Briant for sharing your insight and providing me an inside glimpse into that unique world.

Thanks to Jeremy White for loaning your fireline pack for the cover design team.

Thanks to you, the readers, both near and far—please keep in touch. (shawn@shawngradybooks.com)

And finally:

To all the smokejumpers and wildland firefighters who battle through smoke, heat, and grit to save lives, property, and the environment—from the most remote recesses of our nation to standing between flame fronts and homes—may God bless you and keep you in His abundant grace.

ABOUT THE AUTHOR

SHAWN GRADY has served for over a decade as a firefighter and paramedic in Reno, Nevada, where he lives with his wife and three children. *Booklist* says *Through the Fire* "certainly shows that Grady has promise as an author" and that he "captures the novel's milieu perfectly" in his follow-up thriller, *Tomorrow We Die*—a book *Romantic Times* declares "a definite page-turner."

Visit his Web site at shawngradybooks.com.

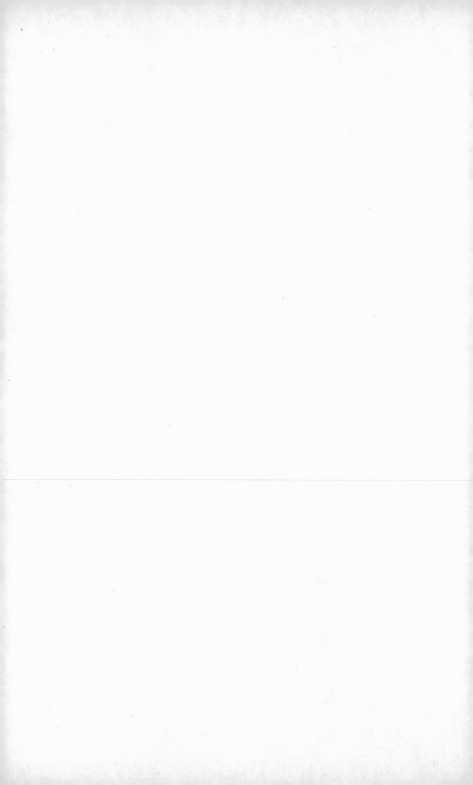